Pewzer's Wake

HELEN BREEDLOVE

iUniverse

PEWZER'S WAKE

Copyright © 2014 Helen Breedlove.

All rights reserved. No part of this book may be used or reproduced by any means, graphic, electronic, or mechanical, including photocopying, recording, taping or by any information storage retrieval system without the written permission of the publisher except in the case of brief quotations embodied in critical articles and reviews.

This is a work of fiction. All of the characters, names, incidents, organizations, and dialogue in this novel are either the products of the author's imagination or are used fictitiously.

iUniverse books may be ordered through booksellers or by contacting:

iUniverse LLC
1663 Liberty Drive
Bloomington, IN 47403
www.iuniverse.com
1-800-Authors (1-800-288-4677)

Because of the dynamic nature of the Internet, any web addresses or links contained in this book may have changed since publication and may no longer be valid. The views expressed in this work are solely those of the author and do not necessarily reflect the views of the publisher, and the publisher hereby disclaims any responsibility for them.

Any people depicted in stock imagery provided by Thinkstock are models, and such images are being used for illustrative purposes only. Certain stock imagery © Thinkstock.

ISBN: 978-1-4917-4174-0 (sc)
ISBN: 978-1-4917-4173-3 (e)

Library of Congress Control Number: 2014913588

Printed in the United States of America.

iUniverse rev. date: 09/09/2014

Chapter 1

THE MURDER

Sheriff LeRoy Chalmer effortlessly drew a long puff on his Marlboro and with raised head exhaled slowly, filling the tiny office with smoke. Across the desk from him sat his young skinny deputy, James McIntire, who was oblivious to the smoke as he tried to work a crossword puzzle from the previous evening's local newspaper. Law enforcement had little to do in Rothersby, the sleepy county seat of no more than two thousand inhabitants. The entire county, located deep in the Ozarks, was sparsely populated.

Jake Hobbs, the jailer, snored loudly in the adjacent room. He sat in one chair and extended his long legs across another chair. With only one man, a regular, in the drunk tank and two men in one of the two cells, there was nothing for him to do except put in his time. He had already fixed them a little grub for breakfast and washed the dishes.

Three other young deputies came in when necessary to fill in when the sheriff was out of town and to work the night shift. Jenkins was the most dependable and the one designated to make any necessary decisions in Chalmer's absence.

The office was a dismal little place with no plaques or pictures on the gray walls. The scuffed tiles on the floor were a darker shade of gray.

Suddenly, the loud boom of a voice jolted the sheriff and his deputy when a man burst through the door. "Ya gotta come quick! It's Ekbert Pewzer! He's dead!" The man heaved in great agony, trying desperately to catch his breath between words. His face was covered with sweat and dirt, and his filthy denim overalls hung loosely on heavy hips.

The slightly potbellied, middle-aged sheriff jumped up, sending his swivel chair spinning backward on its coasters. His startled staccato voice spat out his words in a jumble: "Who's dead? Where? Who are ya anyway? What are ya talkin' about?" McIntire quickly rose to his feet to make room for the distraught man, getting a whiff of the dirty man's body odor as he thrust himself into the compact office.

"He was supposed to bale some hay for me this morning, but didn't show up! That's not like him. He's a sorry sonabitch, but he shows up when he says he's goin' to, so I went over there to tell him what I thought." He wheezed and gasped for air. "I already had the hay down, and with it lookin' like rain, I wanted to get the balin' done, but . . . but he's dead. Deader than a doornail!" He wiped his brow on his tattered chambray shirt.

"Now just have a seat and calm down." Chalmer motioned to the chair McIntire had vacated. The man collapsed his heavy frame into it, ignoring the squeak of protest from the straight-backed chair.

"Now, start at the beginning. First, what's your name?"

"It's George Blackstone, and I'm his nearest neighbor. He's dead-- blood all over the place. His head's bashed in. I never seen anything like it."

"Where do ya live?"

"Way out in the county, south of here."

"Why didn't ya just call us instead of drivin' all the way into town?"

"Didn't ya hear what I said! I live way out--don't have no phone. Do ya want to hear what I've got to say or not?"

"Okay, take it slow and easy. Was he inside the house or outside?" Did ya see any signs of anybody else around his house?"

"The door was wide open, and he was in the livin' room, and I didn't see nobody, but I didn't stop to look. I wanted out of there. I'm not hankerin' to have my head bashed in, so I drove as fast as my old truck'd go to get here."

"Are ya in any shape to show us where his house is? We can follow ya if ya are."

Blackstone's rough hands shook uncontrollably, but he spurted out, "I drove here, didn't I? I reckon I can take ya there, but don't ask me to go in that there house. I don't think I could stand another dose of that awful sight. I'm tellin' ya it's bad--real bad!"

Instantly, Chalmer grabbed his hat, and he and McIntire exited the sheriff's office, which occupied an unkempt brick building next to the county court house. They rushed to the sheriff's car and followed Blackstone down a dusty road toward the far edge of the county. The dust boiled into the un-air-conditioned sheriff's '55 Chevy. "Dammit, all to hell," McIntire grumbled. "Why did this have to happen in our county? Why not in the next county over!"

"Bad luck I guess. Look at it this way. This Blackstone may be a kook. For all we know, his imagination might just be runnin' away with itself. Maybe this didn't even happen. And you need to watch your language."

McIntire brushed his dark crew-cut hair with a swipe of his big hand. The young deputy hadn't signed up for anything like this when he had taken the job as deputy--a job that paid such a small amount that only a single man still living with his folks could afford to tinker with. "Golly durn," he drawled, "I'm not into seein' dead bodies, that's for shore." He tugged at his plaid short-sleeved shirt in an attempt to fan himself, and his unprofessional-looking Levi's seemed to smother him. He was curious. "Did you ever see a murdered person?"

"No, never did, but I guess there's a first time for everything. Now, just don't get in a panic on me." Chalmer was voted in as sheriff, probably because the Democrat running against him was as equally unqualified as he was, and this county overwhelmingly voted Republican.

Much later, they drove past Struthersville, a little town that was also in their county. The school, which would soon see the students trickle in at the start of the school term at the end of the month, stood on the edge of town. It was a decent-looking red brick building, probably built by the WPA during the Depression. McIntire said, more to himself than to the sheriff, "I'm shore glad I don't have to go to school anymore, but I shore feel sorry for them that do."

Following closely behind the fast-driving, frantic Blackstone on the curvy, hilly dirt road made it difficult for the sheriff to see where he was going on this already muggy morning.

Blackstone's truck suddenly made a sharp swerve to the right and rattled to a stop in a gravel driveway with dust swirling up in the sheriff's and deputy's faces as they hurriedly piled out of their car as soon as its squealing brakes brought it to a stop. They looked at the open door to the dilapidated house with an unkempt yard covered with ragweed. A rusty blue truck was parked nearby. "It's all yours, boys. I'm gettin' out of here." Blackstone was backing out of the driveway when the sheriff shouted asking him where he lived. "Right across that there field and over yonder holler." He wasted no time shoving his truck in low and leaving Chalmer and McIntire in the dust and to their own devices to deal with the dead Pewzer. He'd seen enough, and he didn't want any more of it.

His handcuffs dangling from his belt, Chalmer drew his revolver, imitating the scenes he had seen on his newly purchased black and white television set, and cautiously approached the door that stood wide open with flies swarming about. He didn't know why he needed the gun, but it seemed the proper thing to have ready--just in case. Already sneezing from trekking through the ragweed, McIntire followed close behind.

Pewzer's Wake

Inside the house, sure enough, there was the dead Pewzer lying face up, his mutilated head covered with dried blood. The body was already stinking on this sweltering August day in 1956.

McIntire choked back an urge to heave up the coffee and cinnamon roll he'd had for breakfast less than an hour earlier, but Chalmer told him to buck up and act like a man instead of some sissy, although he himself swallowed hard and turned his head several times to avert his eyes from the bloody scene. Each man whipped out a handkerchief from a back pocket.

The forty-one-year-old Chalmer had to prove to McIntire that he was tough like a sheriff should be. He tied the handkerchief over his nose and mouth with shaky hands, knelt besides the body and searched Pewzer's overall pockets, pulling out a wallet that contained a driver's license. Sure enough, this must be Pewzer. The description of height and weight seemed to verify the man's identity. Chalmer wondered if robbery could have been the motive, since there was no cash in the wallet, but the severe beating must have been an act of rage or overkill instead if robbery. If a thief had done this, wouldn't he have just knocked Pewzer in the head, taken his money, and left? He wouldn't have had to beat him to a bloody pulp.

"Looks like somebody was pretty damned mad at this fellow. Whoever he was, he did quite a number on him. Or it could've been more than one."

The sheriff glanced around the filthy room with a few items of clothing strewn about and looked at the dirty ragged furniture. The place must have been begging for a good cleaning for a very long time. The blue speckled linoleum was caked with dried mud, revealing several footprints. A thick layer of dust covered everything. But apparently the house hadn't been ransacked, and nothing seemed to be disturbed. No drawers had been pulled open, and nothing had been turned over, so it wasn't like somebody had been searching for something.

"Just look at all those blood splatters over there," the sheriff gruffly whispered as if he might awaken the dead. The blood was a testament to just how brutal the beating had been. "It sure was a gruesome thing. I wonder what they used--maybe fists with brass knuckles, or maybe some kind of club, but I don't see any club. I don't think bare fists could've done all this," the sheriff speculated further.

McIntire gagged and choked at the grisly scene. "He sure enough has the right name. Pewzer. Pew-ee. I never smelled anything so bad."

"Well, we'd better get the coroner out here. Let's go see if we can get that car radio to work good enough to get a hold of him from here." They both expelled the breath they had been holding as soon as they stepped outside and gulped in the hot air.

Luckily, they were able to get the coroner's office, which was located in the funeral home that Coroner Floyd Manning owned. After Chalmer explained the situation to Manning, as broken up as the message was, the coroner asked for directions and then said he'd be out with the hearse to pick up the body as soon as he could get there.

McIntire scratched his head. "Sheriff, don't ya think that's strange."

"What do ya mean? What's strange?"

"Well, it seems to me that the person that owns the funeral home oughten be the coroner, and the hearse and ambulance oughten serve both purposes."

"You mean you think there's a conflict of interest?"

"Yeah, I guess so, whatever that means."

"Now you're thinkin', my boy. Yep, when there's an accident, and an ambulance is called for, which do you think Manning would rather have on his hands, a person he's supposed to take to the hospital or a body to take the funeral home? Just think about it. Which would make him more money--a patient he may never collect a penny from or a funeral?" Chalmer slowly shook his head up and down, rocking his upper torso in the process. "Yeah, I'd say that's a real conflict of interest, but nobody else ran for coroner, so I guess that's what we're stuck with. Ya know, it's not the best paying job in the world. But anyhow, we don't have to worry about that in this case. That Pewzer fellow in there can't be any deader than he is."

McIntire sneezed. "I hope he don't take long to get here. This ragweed's drivin' me nuts."

"He'll be awhile, so why don't we drive over to Blackstone's house and find out a little more about the stiff in there. Whether we like it or not, it's our job to find out who did this."

Chapter 2

BLACKSTONE

As the men approached Blackstone's farm, they were surprised at how it seemed to stretch endlessly with its fields and wooded areas. In a far field, dairy cows dozed under the shade of an oak tree while others grazed on drought-stricken grass. Calves playfully nudged each other or scurried toward their mother's milk. A few of the cows stood in a murky, mossy pond to cool off. But the men were too worked up to notice.

A foxhound, apparently sore from the previous night's race, lay by the steps to the small front porch of the old two-story house. With a loud bark, another hound came out to greet them.

Blackstone, who had calmed down by this time, came to the door, but he didn't invite them inside. A few white oak trees that stretched toward the cloudless blue sky provided shade for the yard that consisted of dried grass mingled with bare, parched ground. "You fellas look a mite pale. I told ya it was bad. Never seen anything like it."

"What can ya tell us about Pewzer--about any enemies and all?"

"Well, I reckon it'd be easier to tell ya who liked him."

"You mean he wasn't very well liked?"

"No, shore wasn't. Nobody thought much of him. I reckon there won't be anybody very upset 'cause he's gone. Why, one time he even threatened to kill one of my hounds, and I told him straight out that he'd be awful sorry if he did any such thing."

"Did ya ever hear anybody threaten him?"

"No, can't say that I have. At least not recently."

"What do ya mean--not recently?"

"Well, that oldest boy of his--well, it really wasn't his boy--he was his wife's boy, shook his fist at him and told him he'd kill him someday. I can't say as I'd blame him. Old Ekbert just worked him like a mule and then give him a whippin' because he didn't get the plowin' done fast enough. But that was a long time ago."

"Where's this boy now?"

"Don't know. When he got a little bigger, he took off, and I ain't heard from him since."

"What's the kids' names?"

"Well, Davis is the last name. Let's see now. Billy, I think, was his first name, or maybe that was the name of the youngest one. Yeah, one of 'em was Billy and the other one was Alvin."

"You mentioned his wife. Whatever happened to her, and did she have any other kids besides the two boys?"

"Shore enough did--a girl. Name was Mary. They was all by her first husband, and then she had a little girl by Pewzer. I don't remember her name."

"Do you know where any of 'em are now?"

"Well, I hear tell that the wife--Opal was her name--just up and left one day--took the kids with her. They were teenagers then, except for the little girl. One boy still lives around here, maybe in the next county over. And the girls, I think they live in Struthersville, least ways I seen 'em there, but I don't know for shore. They're probably gettin' up close to thirty by now--except the young one, and I reckon she'd probably be in her twenties." Blackstone propped himself up by a wobbly porch post and rubbed his whiskered chin. "Ekbert treated the youngest boy like he did the oldest one, and I always figured he did things to the girl, if ya know what I mean. She was

9

always just as fluttery as a little bird that had fell out of the nest. He was a mean sonabitch."

"You mean he sexually abused her?"

"Now, mind you, I don't have no proof of that, but that's just the way I seen it."

"Do ya think he abused the youngest one, his own daughter?"

"Now, that I can't say for shore, but what do you think? Use your head. Don't ya think if he came on to one, don't ya figure he did the same to the other one? Maybe Opal got enough of it, and that's why she left. I don't know. I don't know nothing for shore, mind ya."

Chalmer stuck out his hand and shook Blackstone's callused, dirty hand to thank him. "You've been a big help, and we'll want to talk to you again about other folks he had any contact with, but right now, we'd better get back over there and wait for the ambulance . . . or maybe I should say the hearse." Chalmer started toward the car, then turned back. "Do ya know any places he liked to go to, where he hung out, or anything like that?"

"Well, let's see now. I heard him talkin' about goin' to Susie's Bar and Grill in Rothersby a few times. That's the only place I know about, except for Struthersville. He went there a lot and was always botherin' people."

"What do ya mean by that?"

"You know, pickin' on 'em, makin' 'em miserable. Pewzer was good at that--'bout the only thing he was good at, except for balin' hay. He did that real good."

"By the way, what do ya think will happen to Pewzer's livestock? It seems they ought to at least be checked on."

"I'll see to 'em till somethin' can be done about 'em. I shore think more of them horses and cows--even the pigs--than I did Ekbert."

"Well, that'd be good of ya. And thanks again. We'll be in touch."

Chapter 3

THE HEARSE

When the middle-aged, neatly dressed Manning arrived with the hearse, he brushed his hands together and took one look at the body. His first comment was "Yep, he's dead all right--murdered I'd say." His squeaky, feminine voice didn't seem to be compatible with his tall, robust body.

McIntire rolled his eyes upward in disbelief. "Now I'd say it don't take no genius to figure that out. I reckon he didn't do that to hisself. You'd have to be dumber than a stump to think anything different."

Manning glared at McIntire with his beady eyes, giving him a non-verbal warning to mind his own business. "I just hope he's got enough money in the bank to pay for his funeral. I wonder where he did his banking."

Chalmer grinned, thinking how good it would be if Manning didn't get his money, but he said, "Seems he ought to have enough with this big farm and all. I wonder who'll end up with it. That's something we'll have to think about--might be a motive, ya know."

Pulling a stretcher out of the back of the black hearse that was now covered with dust, Manning eyed McIntire with a sharp smirk. "You look like a strapping big fella--kinda skinny, but big enough to be of some help. Give me a hand getting this guy in the hearse."

"Why me? That's your job."

"Well," Manning said mockingly, "you're dumber than a stump if you think I can do this by myself."

The sheriff signaled with a toss of his head for McIntire to do as he was asked.

McIntire quickly grabbed Pewzer's lifeless feet, knowing there was no way he could handle that emaciated head. That was a coroner's job! At least he wouldn't have to touch any skin--only the dirty boots. After the body was half-carried, half-dragged and heaved onto the stretcher, he turned his head and retched while trying to keep the vomit from coming up in his throat.

As soon as they had loaded the stretcher carrying Pewzer's bloody body into the back of the hearse and Manning drove off, Chalmer shook his head. "Consider yourself lucky, my boy. How would ya like to smell that all the way back to town? There's not enough money to make up for that." He looked up at the blazing sun that was high in the heavens by this time. "Right now, we'd better head back to town, make some phone calls, and eat some lunch."

McIntire thought his boss must have a stomach of a starving wolf to even think about lunch after the rot-gut stuff they'd dealt with, but he didn't argue. They climbed into the car and started the dusty drive back to the sheriff's office.

After eating a hamburger with lots of onions at a cafe, locally called the Greasy Spoon, Chalmer scanned the area's phone books for a Billy or Alvin Davis. "Bingo! Here's an Alvin Davis. Address is in Oatland. That's just over in the next county. I probably wouldn't be lucky enough to catch anybody at home at this time of the day."

He dialed the number and to his surprise a woman answered the phone. "This is Sheriff Chalmer, and I need to speak to Alvin Davis, please."

"Is something wrong? I'm his wife," a meek voice muttered.

"No, I guess you wouldn't say so."

"Then why do you need to speak to Alvin?"

"Well, I just needed to touch bases with him about an important matter."

"Can't you tell me what this is all about?"

"Well, I'd rather talk to your husband about that." Chalmer hoped she wasn't one of those women who took offense at being treated like she wasn't smart enough to know anything, but in this case he needed to talk to Ekbert's stepson instead of her. He wasn't about to tell her Ekbert was murdered. He wanted to surprise Alvin with that information--if indeed, it was a surprise to him. Right at this moment everyone was a suspect--especially a family member who probably hated him and had every right to. But why would any of them kill him after all these years?

"He's at work right now--down at the shoe factory, but I expect him back about six. You can call back then."

"I appreciate that ma'am, but if it's all the same to you, me and my deputy'll just come by and talk to him eyeball to eyeball." Chalmer paused. "By the way, can you tell me where his mother lives?"

By this time there was a hesitancy in her voice, a slight note of skepticism and maybe a bit of anger, but she begrudgingly said, "Yeah, she lives in Springfield."

"Does she work any place?"

"Yeah, she works at Clinger Department Store--got a real good job, but what's that to you anyway?"

"Not much I guess. Well, thank ya, ma'am." He put the receiver down.

He looked at McIntire who continued to sneeze from the effects of the ragweed and to work on the crossword puzzle he had started what seemed to him like a lifetime ago. He wasn't making much progress, never did, but he continued to make an effort anyway.

"Come on, McIntire. We've got some questions to ask." Chalmer slapped him on the back and rubbed out a stub of a cigarette in the ashtray. "Before we get finished, you'll wished you'd had a bite to eat."

"Where we goin'?"

"Susie's Bar and Grill. That's where."

Chapter 4

SUSIE'S BAR AND GRILL

Inside the bar, thick smoke curled through the air to mix with the choking smell of stale grease. McIntire coughed, but Chalmer laughed and patted his chest to make sure his badge was in plain view. "You're a little young to be in a place like this, McIntire, but ya won't get educated any younger. Let's go see what we can find out."

The bar was empty except for a couple seated off to one side in a dark corner. They were whispering and laughing, oblivious to everything and everybody around them. The man reached over and smugly pinched the woman on her right breast. She momentarily fixed her gaze on his lustful face, giggled, and brushed his hand away.

When Chalmer and McIntire stepped up to the bar, they were greeted by a burly proprietor with a thick mustache and black hair that curled into the collar of his blue, well-worn shirt. He also served as the bartender. Chalmer wondered why the place was called Susie's and if a Susie actually owned most of it, but that was no concern of his. That wasn't why he was here. "What can I do for you, sheriff?"

McIntire, his hormones raging, didn't hear the question. He was too busy staring at the large semi-nude picture of a shapely woman that graced the area behind the bar. He was so enthralled that he could hardly breathe.

Pewzer's Wake

"I understand that a guy named Ekbert Pewzer used to come in here some," Chalmer said. "I thought maybe ya might tell me when ya last saw him and if he was ever with anybody."

"Oh, you're investigatin' his murder, huh?"

"You know about that already?" Chalmer knew that news traveled fast in this town, but he didn't realize just how fast.

"Yeah, it didn't take the town criers long to find that out as soon as they saw that hearse rollin' into town. Some of them fellas make it their business to know everything, and it's not long before all of us know about it, so I've already been thinkin' about the last time he was in here." The chatty bartender paused long enough to wipe the counter that didn't need wiping while Chalmer waited for him to continue. "It was Saturday night. He had a beer or two, and then two other guys weasled their way up on each side of him and started drinkin' a shot of whisky and buyin' Pewzer one drink after another. They were pretty free with their cash, and that's sure good for business." He grinned, revealing white teeth beneath his dark sloppily trimmed mustache. "Well, pretty soon, Pewzer was drunk as a skunk and they offered to see that he got home. They all left together, and I ain't seen any of 'em since."

Chalmer's eyes lit up and with raised eyebrows asked, "Did ya know these men?"

"Nope, never saw 'em before. But there was somethin' about 'em that struck me as strange."

"Oh? What's that?"

"Well, it looked like one guy was maybe wearin' a wig and the other one maybe had wrinkles where they weren't supposed to be and a tooth blacked out."

"You mean they were tryin' to disguise their looks? Maybe so as nobody would recognize them again?"

"Yeah, that's it, but maybe I'm just imaginin' things after what happened to Pewzer. You know, your mind can pull funny tricks on ya sometimes. But they kinda reminded me of two guys I saw when I took the garbage out back about a week before that--about the same size and all. They were hangin' out in a car like they was waitin' for somebody. Later, I saw 'em talkin' to some woman."

By this time, McIntire was fully alert even though he was still ogling the picture and his stomach was growling from hunger. His eyes finally skittered away from the picture to look at Chalmer. He couldn't believe he was helping with a murder investigation. In his mind he was trying to piece together all the information that he was hearing--attempting to make some sense out of all of it.

"What did the woman look like?"

"Didn't pay no attention to her."

"Well, was she skinny or fat or ugly or good lookin'? What?"

"Can't say. Like I said, I didn't pay any attention. Maybe she was kinda light headed."

When the sheriff and his deputy left, they didn't speak for a few minutes. Finally the silence got the best of McIntire. "Sheriff, are you thinkin' what I'm thinkin'?"

"I don't know. What are you thinkin'?"

"Shucks, it appears to me that a woman wouldn't be strong enough to beat up Pewzer, but she shore could pay somebody to do it for her--that is, if she had the money." McIntire was proud of his reasoning. "What do you think?"

"I think you're right. And don't forget--a man could have paid somebody just as easy. Anybody with enough money could have had it done." Chalmer rubbed his chin. "I wonder who'll get Pewzer's farm now that he's dead. You know what they say about revenge and money being great motivators."

"Bein' great what?"

"Motivators. You know, a reason for doin' somethin'."

"Yeah, even murder."

"McIntire, we've got our work cut out for us."

The young deputy's gangling frame stood a little taller at being included in the work ahead.

"Let's go back to the office and see if we can get a hold of Opal Pewzer at that Clinger Department Store. I need to tell her about this before she hears it from somebody else. Besides, I want to know how she reacts. Or maybe she already knows about it. I suppose she had a good reason to do Pewzer in, especially if he molested her daughters. I don't have any use for that type--none at all."

"What type?"

"You know--the kind that bothers little girls. They ought to string every one of 'em up by their balls."

"Golly durn! That'd hurt."

"That's the whole point."

Chalmer drove in silence back toward his office. With his lips set in a grim line, he had a lot on his mind. It wouldn't be easy finding the killer or killers and having enough evidence to get a conviction. Defense lawyers could be pretty slick. But he was jumping the gun. He didn't have the foggiest idea about a logical suspect.

Chapter 5

OPAL DAVIS

When a manager at the department store came to the phone, Chalmer explained that he was a sheriff and asked if it would be a convenient time for him to speak to Opal Pewzer.

"I'm sorry. Who did you say? We don't have an Opal Pewzer working here."

"Oh, I was told that she was one of your employees."

"You must've been given the wrong information. The only Opal that we have is Opal Davis."

Chalmer nearly dropped the receiver, but after a stunned silence, said, "I guess that's the woman I need to speak to. Could you have her come to the phone for me?"

After only a few moments had passed, Opal answered the phone with a questioning hello. Her voice was pleasant, almost melodious.

"This is Sheriff Chalmer, Miss Davis. I have information about your ex-husband."

"My ex-husband? What are you talking about?" Her voice had instantly turned to a sharp growl.

"Uh, Ekbert Pewzer."

"For your information, he's not my ex-husband. I was never married to the bastard--except maybe by common law," she snapped. She hesitated a few seconds before reluctantly spewing forth with more information. "I lived with him for many years and gave birth to his daughter." Bitterness emanated from her spiteful voice. "What information about the old bastard could I possibly be interested in?"

"Maybe you won't be interested, but Pewzer got himself murdered." Chalmer was careful not to reveal where, when, or how he was murdered. He hoped she might say something that would implicate herself in some way or another. He had followed those television detective stories carefully, and knew this was the slick way to handle matters such as this.

There was a long pause; then she said, "Good. Somebody finally gave him what he deserved."

"I take it you weren't very fond of him."

She laughed. It sounded more like a scoff. "That's right. I wasn't. I hated his guts."

"Then do you mind telling me why you lived with him for so long?"

"Now that's not any of your business, is it?"

"No, ma'am, it's not. I was just curious." Chalmer wanted to keep her talking as long as he could.

"Well, Mr. Sheriff, what's a woman to do when she's got three kids to raise and no way to feed them? You figure it out! Now, I've got to get back to work."

"Just one more minute, ma'am. I need to know where you've been the last couple of days and whether you'd been down in this neck of the woods. It'd help in the investigation."

"Now where do you think I've been? I've been right here in Springfield and reporting to work every day."

"Can anybody verify that?"

"Yeah, my boss. He's standing right here, and he's wondering what a sheriff wants with me. Do you want to talk to him?"

"Naw, that won't be necessary. But before you hang up, can ya tell me where your son Billy lives? I need to talk with him. I already know where your other kids live."

Helen Breedlove

"No, I can't tell you where Billy lives. Now I've got to get back to work before I get fired." She slammed the receiver down so hard that Chalmer smacked his hand across his ear.

After he'd filled his young deputy in on the conversation, McIntire asked, "Don't ya think it's kinda odd that she didn't ask how he was murdered?"

"Real odd--unless she already knows. And don't ya think it's kinda odd that she didn't know where her own son lives?"

Chapter 6

ALVIN DAVIS

Chalmer scratched his thinning head of hair and then rubbed his chin. "Let's go talk to Alvin Davis," he said to McIntire. "He should be home from work by now. Maybe he'll shed some light on things." He called out to the jailer to keep an eye on things while they drove over to the next county. About all the jailer would have to do is answer the phone.

Alvin and his pretty wife lived in a small but well-kept bungalow on a street of similar houses. Alvin, with a puzzled look on his ruddy face, came to the door and reluctantly invited the two law enforcement men in after they had introduced themselves. Three cautious adolescents stared curiously at them. "If you don't mind, we'd like to ask you a few questions about Ekbert Pewzer," the sheriff said before being seated on a brown fake leather sofa.

Alvin wrinkled his brow, bit his lower lip, and then asked, "What about the old bastard? Did he kill somebody?"

"Uh, not exactly. It was the other way around."

"What do you mean?"

"Somebody did a number on him--bashed his head in. He's dead."

Alvin eyed the sheriff with skepticism and bit his lower lip. "Well good--couldn't happen to a nicer guy," he huffed sardonically and with more than just a little animosity and bitterness.

"Do ya know of anybody who might have wanted to do him in?"

"Who didn't! Everybody hated him, me included. I won't deny that, but if you're wondering if I had anything to do with this, you're wrong. I probably should have done it myself a long time ago, but no, I didn't have anything to do with it. Unfortunately, I didn't have the guts." Alvin glanced at his wife and kids, a boy and two girls, hesitated, and then asked, "When and where did it happen?"

"Just a few days ago. His neighbor, George Blackstone, found him dead in his living room."

"Good ol' George, huh? I don't see how he put up with him, but he was always a patient kind of fellow--always good to me. I bet he won't miss him any."

"Do ya have any idea what'll happen to the farm now that Pewzer's dead?"

Alvin thought for a few seconds and then shook his head as if trying to answer that question. He cleared his throat. "I don't reckon he's got any kin, except for Louella. She's his real daughter, you know, but he's such a mean SOB I doubt that he'd leave the farm to her--probably thought he'd take it with him when he died--if he even thought he'd ever die."

Chalmer and McIntire listened, watching every hand gesture and every facial expression. McIntire imagined he was a real detective, picking up any clues from this man, one of the probable suspects.

"She'll be the one that more than likely gets the place, but of course, it'll have to go through probate," Chalmer speculated. "A greedy lawyer will get a chunk of whatever it's worth--always do." He looked for any reaction from Alvin as he said that, but the man didn't even blink an eye. "And of course, the undertaker'll have to be paid. He rubbed his chin. "By the way, can ya tell me where your brother Billy lives?

After a long pause, Alvin said, "No. Sorry, I can't."

The sheriff thanked Alvin for his time, and he and McIntire were on their way back to Rothersby.

Determined to solve his first murder case, the sheriff decided to pay another visit to George Blackstone the next day. "Ya never know what he might be hidin'," he told his deputy. "Who knows. Maybe he was just fakin' it when he came in here the other day all upset. Maybe he's the one that did the deed."

Chapter 7

MOLASSES MAKING

When they pulled up to Blackstone's place, there was a lot of activity with kids and grownups bustling about. "Golly durn, what's goin' on here?" McIntire asked, referring to an enormous contraption and a horse going around and around circling it.

"Well, I'll be damn, if they're not makin' molasses. I didn't know anybody did that anymore. Boy, you're in for a real education," Chalmer declared.

Four or five kids were running around sucking on juicy cane stalks. A horse, apparently the mate to the one that was going in circles, poked his head over the fence, almost begging for a stalk. The youngest one accommodated him by handing him a stalk and giving him a pet on his velvety nose.

The men approached the enormous juicer that was being fed cane stalks by someone Chalmer didn't recognize. A tired old chestnut horse plodded round and round to squeeze the juice out of the sugar cane, where it was directed into a huge vat set up on big rocks with a fire blazing under it. A boy of about fourteen, his shirtless upper torso wet with sweat, stoked the fire to keep it hot on this sultry day as the juice came to a boil to make molasses. Younger children dipped their stalks into the foam and gleefully licked it off after blowing on it to cool it down. It was almost like a celebration.

Wide-eyed, Deputy McIntire took it all in before asking Blackstone a question. "Don't that there horse get dizzy? How long's he been doin' that anyhow?"

"If he does, he don't say so. You don't hear him complainin', do ya?"

The other man walked up and introduced himself. "I'm Chester Morgan--live just a mile south of here. And I can see by your badge, you're the sheriff."

"Sure am. LeRoy Chalmer's the name, and this here's my deputy, James McIntire."

The men shook hands before Chalmer said he'd like to ask both men some questions, just to get things straight. "You wouldn't know anything about Pewzer's death, now would ya?" Chalmer asked Morgan, a tall, deeply tanned man, who sported muscles like those of a heavy-weight boxer.

"Are ya askin' if'n I had anything to do with it? Well, shore 'nough didn't, but I wouldn't have raised a finger to help him, and he got what he deserved. I hated the son of a bitch. Why, one time I saw him nearly beat Opal's oldest boy to death. His name's Billy. He'd have probably killed him if'n I hadn't come a long and pulled him off. Another time after the oldest one run off, the youngest boy--his name's Alvin--was down by that low water bridge skippin' rocks across a pool of water with my oldest boy--he's all growed up nowadays--and ol' Ekbert come runnin' at 'em with a club. He hit Alvin real hard across the back and told him to get back to plowin'. Then he threatened to do the same to my boy just as I walked up on 'em. I told him I'd kill him if'n he ever threatened my boy again. I would've too, but no, I didn't kill the bastard, but I'm glad he's dead. He weren't no good to nobody, and whoever did it deserves a medal." Suddenly he stopped talking and focused on a small girl and boy. "You two be careful around that fire, hear?" Then turning back to Chalmer, he said, "Them kids of mine love molasses makin' time. Well, I guess we all do. I furnish the sugar cane, and George here furnishes the equipment. The only trouble is we have so much molasses we don't know what to do with it all. You can be sure if Ekbert was still alive, he'd be down here to get some of it. It was hard to tell him he couldn't have any, so we always gave him a little, but we'd have rather fed it to the hogs. Hogs like molasses, ya know, and when ya have a lot of it, it'll just turn to sugar before ya can use it all." He scratched his full head of dark hair. "If'n you'll stay awhile, we'll give ya some of it."

That was when Blackstone, who had been too busy with his horse to get in on the conversation, asked, "What brings ya down this way anyhow? I've already told ya all I know about that sorry Ekbert."

"Well, we thought maybe ya might have thought of somethin' since we were here the last time."

"Naw, I told ya all I know."

"What about some other people around here? Can ya tell us about them--any grudges and all?"

Chester Morgan spoke up. "That'd be anybody that ever knowed him. Ever'body had some kind of grudge or 'nother against Pewzer. Like I said, he was a no-good bastard. Why, old timers in these parts used to claim he even poisoned his own mother to get his rotten hands on that big old farm."

Chalmer frowned. "Nice guy, huh?" He turned to walk away. "Well, thanks for the information."

"Wait a minute," George Blackstone broke in. "I jest remembered Pewzer was married to another woman a long time before Opal. They had a boy, but then she left him. Knowin' Pewzer, I figured he was mean to her, and one day she jest up and left."

"And what was her name before she married Pewzer?"

"Well, it's been a long time ago, but I think it was Jolene Fairway, or somethin' or the other like that."

"Do you know what ever happened to her and her boy?"

"Well, it seems like I heard one time that she got real sick, but I'm not positive about that."

"Do ya know what happened to the boy?"

"No, shore don't."

Chalmer muddled that over in his brain before saying, "You wouldn't happen to know where Pewzer did his bankin', would ya? That funeral director's eager to know about that."

"Well, ever'body in these parts banks over at Struthersville. It'd be a lot closer than goin' all the way into Rothersby."

"Well, thanks for the help. I appreciate it, and I'm glad to see somebody still makes molasses. I've not seen that done since I was a kid."

Being not more than a kid himself, McIntire stuck a cane stalk in the foamy mixture, blew on it, and licked it as he and the sheriff got back in the car.

Chalmer scratched his head and chewed on the side of his jaw. "You'd think there's somebody that's sorry Pewzer's dead."

"Do you reckon he had a girlfriend--maybe a married one?" McIntire was trying his best to be helpful. "Maybe a jealous husband did him in. Do ya think so, uh?"

"Are you kiddin'? What woman--even an old hag--would have anything to do with Ekbert Pewzer?"

"Well, we know that two women did at one time. Maybe he could turn on the charm for a little sex." McIntire felt somewhat manly discussing sex with his boss.

Biting back a grin, Chalmer gave McIntire a disgusted look and said, "Let's stop in Struthersville on our way back to the office. It'd be interesting to see if Pewzer had any money, and if he did, who might end up with it now that he's dead."

When they drove into Struthersville, a sleepy little town that the world had left behind long ago, they were shocked to see a large gathering in the middle of the graveled street that separated the few businesses. On one side of Main Street stood a grocery store, a doctor's office with the door wide open and nobody about, a post office, a barbershop, and a gas station just across the railroad track. Farther down, a train depot was snuggled up against the railroad track. On the other side, there was another grocery store, a drug store, a cracker box of a ladies' apparel store, a cafe, a bank, and a feed store. A blacksmith shop marked the very end of the street. They had driven past a school and two churches on opposite ends of town as they approached Main Street.

"Hey, there's some kind of celebration goin' on," McIntyre exclaimed, as he saw the raucous crowd. In the middle of the street, people shouted, jumped up and down, danced and laughed despite the oppressive heat. "I wonder what that's all about."

The shouting stopped when they saw the approaching sheriff's car, and the revelers parted to let the car go through as it made its way to park in front of the bank.

Chapter 8

THE BANKER

When they walked into the bank, a tall structure with shiny floors and countertops, a man dressed in a light blue suit and striped tie rose from a large, elaborately carved desk to greet them. A ceiling fan whirred above him. "Well, to what do I owe the honor of this visit from the sheriff?" The tall man with a receding hairline and a big nose with flared nostrils proudly puffed out his chest and extended his hand. McIntire thought he must be crazy to be spiffed up like that on this terribly muggy day when nobody else gave a rip what they looked like, just as long as they staved off the heat. He was impressed with the high ceilings and pleasant smell.

After shaking the soft hand of Banker Floyd Calvin, Sheriff Chalmer said, "We need some answers that we think you can help us with."

"What's that? I'm always ready to serve," but he hastily added with a chuckle, "I'll do anything that's within the law."

"Well, for starters, you can tell us what all that commotion out in the street is about."

"Oh, that. People are celebrating Ekbert Pewzer's death. They've been at it for hours. Even people that live out of town are coming in to join the festivities."

"I take it, he wasn't very well liked."

"That's an understatement."

"And that brings us to our bigger question. Did he have a bank account here?"

"Yes, he did. Sure enough."

"That's good to know. I reckon that undertaker'll get his money after all. He was worried about that." Chalmer rubbed his chin for a few seconds wondering who could profit the most from Pewzer's murder, and then asked, "Was anybody else's name on that bank account?"

"Well, not actually, but I convinced him to designate someone to receive it in case of his death. He got mad and cussed up a storm at such a suggestion, but when I told him someone would need to be able to pay for his funeral someday, that nobody lived forever, he reluctantly acquiesced." Calvin held his head a little higher at using such an important sounding word, probably hoping no one would understand. Chalmer thought he probably ought to use a few big words of his own. He didn't want anybody thinking he was stupid. Maybe it was time to counter the banker's big word with a few he kept recorded in his little notebook, but he decided to save them for another day.

"He what?" McIntire asked.

"You know. He gave in." Chalmer said, almost embarrassed that McIntire would show his stupidity by asking such a question. He looked again at Calvin. "And what was the name of the designated person?"

"That was Louella Pewzer, his real daughter. I guess she's the one who'll have to make funeral arrangements.

"Do ya know where she lives?"

"Well, as a matter of fact, I do. She lives right here in Struthersville-- over on Walnut Street, just a block over from Main Street. It's the house with the red shutters. You can't miss it."

"Then I guess we'd better go tell her she needs to make funeral arrangements. We can't leave Pewzer to rot, and I'm sure the funeral home in Rothersby will be glad to dispose of the matter." Chalmer didn't intentionally use the word *dispose*, but he chuckled to himself anyway. "Thanks for your help."

When they walked back to the car, McIntire, sweating profusely, exclaimed, "Golly durn, my mouth's so dry my tongue's stickin' to the roof of my mouth. I gotta have somethin' to drink."

"Me too," the sheriff said. "Let's go see if we can get a soda pop over at that cafe. What do ya want?"

"I'll take a Grapette." McIntire actually wanted two of the little bottles of pop, but was too ashamed to ask for them.

After McIntire had swallowed his Grapette in just a few gulps and Chalmer finished off his Coke, they left the bottles and were on their way to Louella Pewzer's house.

Chapter 9

LOUELLA PEWZER

With McIntire at his side, Chalmer took one last drag off his cigarette, dropped it to the ground, and stomped it out before climbing the steps to the house on Walnut Street. With the strong scent of a few marigolds alongside the house struggling to survive in the heat, McIntire sneezed.

The screen was the only thing standing between them and the buzz of a fan inside. An attractive blonde with violet eyes answered their knock on the door of the well-kept house.

"What can I do for you gentlemen?" Louella asked innocently when she saw the sheriff's badge, maybe too innocently, Chalmer thought.

As for McIntire, his heart was thumping hard against his rib cage. Like most eighteen-year-olds, he was turned on by a sexy-looking shape like hers, and he looked her up and down, taking in all the curves decked out in a light green tank top and tan pedal-pushers. He was also impressed by the way she regally carried herself as if she was someone special and very well knew it.

But Chalmer was all business. "We understand that you're now the sole owner of Ekbert Pewzer's bank account."

"Oh? I didn't know that," she responded with the same kind of innocence.

"Yeah, that's what the banker said, and I guess you'll have to be the one to take care of his funeral and pay for your dad's burial."

"Where is he now? And don't call him my dad!"

McIntire looked puzzled. "He's dead. That's where he is."

Chalmer gave him a withering look. "She knows that, numbskull. She wants to know where his *body* is."

"Oh," McIntire said with a chagrined expression, his gaze dropping to the slats of the porch. He didn't like being dressed down in front of a beautiful woman.

"He's at the funeral home in Rothersby," the sheriff said. "He's been embalmed, but they're not eager to keep him. They think it'd cause too much of a spectacle when decent people are havin' visitations for their folks."

"It'd be all right with me if they can bring him down here. I don't think I'd care to go all the way into Rothersby for the old dead bastard. We'll have his wake here."

"Here in Struthersville? Where?"

"Down at the end of Main Street at Filber's Grocery Store."

"A grocery store! A funeral home in a grocery store? A furniture store, yes, but a grocery store? I never heard the like."

"Golly durn!" McIntire gasped.

"Old man Filber's got one in the back of the store, right next to the meat counter."

Forgetting all about Louella's curves, Mcntire's eyes popped open wide. "You're kiddin'!"

"No, I'm not." Louella laughed, enjoying her revelation. "But there's a thin little wall that separates the corpses from the meat."

McIntire nearly gagged. He thought he might be sick, but Chalmer kept a poker face.

"Can you go with me to ask Filber if we can lay him out there overnight?" she asked in a treacly way that made it hard to refuse. "He won't be happy about it, but it'd just be a short way to the Struthersville cemetery from there. I figure the quicker he's six feet under the better for everybody."

"You didn't think much of your father, did ya?" Chalmer asked, always searching for a plausible suspect. Louella was close to the top of his list. After all, she was going to make a lot of money as a result of his death.

"I hated him. For all I care, you could dump him in a ditch and let the buzzards pick him to pieces."

"If ya want to go to that grocery store now, we'll go with ya. If it's okay with this Filber fella, I'll call the funeral home in Rothersby and have them bring him down."

"Then that's settled," Louella said. "Like I said, the sooner I get this over with, the better."

"And the sooner I can solve this murder, the better," Chalmer said, watching Louella for any suspicious eye movement or gesture. He congratulated himself for being pretty good at observing people without them being aware of it. "You can settle up with the funeral home in Rothersby later."

Chapter 10

FILBER'S GROCERY STORE

When they pushed open a squeaky door to the dirty grocery store, the odor of a litter box that hadn't been emptied for several weeks assailed them. Two gray striped cats let out a screeching meow, and one jumped up on a huge butcher's block that had been there, probably unscrubbed, for at least a half a century. No customers were anywhere about.

McIntire frowned, and out of the side of his mouth whispered, "How'd you like to have some lunch meat sliced on that?"

The rest of the store wasn't much better. Some of the canned goods were covered with dust, and one can was even bulging at the top, ready to explode, making McIntire wonder how many people this store had poisoned. The place hadn't had a fresh coat of paint in heaven knows when. He could see why the place had no customers, especially with another grocery store in town.

At his desk sitting behind the cash register with one leg extended, Filber had his pant leg rolled up and was giving himself a shot. He looked up, first at Louella Pewzer, and then at the sheriff and the deputy. "Insulin, you know. I gotta have it."

Chalmer knew about that because he had a good friend who was a diabetic so it didn't bother him, but the shot made McIntire squeamish. He turned his head aside to avoid witnessing the injection.

"Can I help you with something?" Filber asked after slowly tending to his injection and rolling his pant leg down.

"I've got a big favor to ask of you," Louella said almost apologetically with a flutter of her long eyelashes as she tried her best to turn on the charm, an accomplishment she was good at and clearly proud of.

"What's that?"

"Is it all right if we have Ekbert Pewzer's wake in your back room there, just for the evening of course?" she asked, pointing in the direction of the make-shift funeral parlor. "I know you sometime keep the dead there until they can be taken to the cemetery."

Filber's baggy eyes snapped. "Now why would I do that? The old sonabitch never did anything for me." His face turned red all the way up to his bald scalp, and he began shaking. "One time he came in here when I was gettin' ready to give myself a shot. He grabbed the needle out of my hand and squirted the insulin all over my head and laughed like a jackass. You'd have thought it was the funniest thing he ever did see. I hope he rots in hell."

Listening to the sad commentary, Chalmer shook his head. "Well, wouldn't it give ya some satisfaction to know ya got the last laugh with him laid out here with his head all bashed in? Besides I'm sure Louella would pay ya for your trouble."

The greedy Filber frowned and thought about that for a few seconds. "I guess it might be okay. Business hasn't been too good lately." McIntire's eyes shot open as if to say *I wonder why?*

Proud that he'd made such a convincing argument, Chalmer said, "Then if it's all right, we'll have the funeral home in Rothersby bring him down. He's already been embalmed."

"Yeah, I reckon it'd be okay. They can lay him out in there," Filber said, pointing toward the back. "But I doubt anybody'd come to pay their respects. Well, maybe out of curiosity or to celebrate a little, and maybe when they come in, they'll buy some groceries."

Again, McIntire thought of how stupid it would be for anybody to buy groceries in this rat hole. He started to say something, but the words died on his lips.

Chalmer and McIntire walked out of the store with Louella, pleased with what they'd accomplished. "By the way, Louella, where does your sister live? We probably need to talk to her too," the sheriff said.

She shook her head sorrowfully. "Is that absolutely necessary? She's not in very good health."

"Well, we have to touch all the bases. I'm sure you can understand that."

"I'm sure you do, not that anybody'd care if you never found out who did him in. She lives just a few houses down from me, but she's not home today. She had a doctor's appointment in Rothersby. A friend took her."

"By the way, how come you were home today? You do have a job, don't ya?"

Chalmer was wondering if she had enough money on hand to pay a killer.

"Oh, I have a job all right--at the gold fish hatchery a few miles from here, but it's a sorry one. I'm on vacation for a couple weeks."

"They pay ya for a vacation?"

"Yeah, a little anyway, and they ought to, no more than they pay us?"

"What do ya do there?"

"Sort fish."

Chalmer had no idea what that involved or why fish needed to be sorted. But he had seen big cans of fish by Struthersville's depot, waiting to be shipped out by train. "Well, we'll probably see ya tonight at the wake."

"Don't hold your breath. I won't be there."

"By the way, where does your brother Billy live? Does he live in these parts or thereabouts?" Chalmer asked, noticing that when he did so, Louella's eyes shifted away uncomfortably.

She answered, "Can't say. I haven't been in touch with him for quite some time."

Chalmer detected an uncertainty in her voice and thought she might be lying, but he turned his attention to McIntire. "I'll make that phone call, and I'll also call my back-up deputy to hold down the fort at the office until Jenkins gets there. There's no need for us to drive all the way back. It's not like I've got a wife waitin' for me anymore." He sighed regretfully. His wife of fifteen years had divorced him eight months earlier. "I want to be here when people come to see Pewzer all laid out--to see who comes and if anybody cares," Chalmer said. "Maybe the killer'll be here. You know what they say about a killer."

"No, what?" McIntire asked, as confused as ever.

"I heard on a television program that killers always return to the scene of the crime."

"But this ain't the scene."

Chalmer threw up his hands and said with disgust, "Don't ya think I know that! But it's the next best thing to it."

"Oh." But McIntire still didn't get the connection.

"Let's get a bite to eat while we're waitin' for Pewzer's body," Chalmer suggested, as he looked up and down the sorry little town.

Now over his shock at seeing the dirty butcher's block, McIntire had a suggestion of his own. "Maybe we could get Filber to cut us some baloney and make us a sandwich."

Chalmer's jaw dropped and he glared at McIntire.

"Aw shucks, I was just funnin'," he said. They walked across the street and entered a greasy spoon of a cafe. They thought about ordering a ham sandwich, but soon decided against it when they speculated that the ham could have been cut on Filber's butcher's block. Instead, they ordered a hamburger with lots of onions.

Chapter 11

THE VIEWING AND BURIAL

At dusk, Chalmer and McIntire were seated off to one side in metal folding chairs in Filber's backroom, a dismal place with dirty walls and only one picture--that of Jesus Christ nailed to the cross. Hoping to get a list of plausible suspects, they observed the reaction of the "mourners" as they filed past Pewzer's casket. Most of the people who came in were probably just curious or just wanted to be assured that Pewzer's head had been bashed in. Or maybe it was that strange desire to look at the dead. Most of them quickly filed out, and there was no hint of a suspect. Louella was noticeably absent as were Pewzer's so-called stepchildren.

The mortuary had done a reasonably good job of patching Pewzer's face up considering what they had to work with. Chalmer wondered how they did that, and at the same time was glad he didn't have to work in a funeral home that embalmed the dead.

Right before closing up shop for the evening, a wiry old man with a gray beard stumbled in, leaned over the open casket, and stared for a long time at the corpse in the cheap coffin, which wasn't much better than a pine box. He seemed to have a lot on his mind.

Chalmer whispered to McIntire, "Well, maybe everybody's been wrong. Maybe that's one person that liked Pewzer."

Just then, the man coughed and spit a huge chaw of tobacco into the restored face of the corpse.

Startled, both lawmen jumped up from their chairs, with McIntire knocking his over with a loud thud of metal against the concrete floor, and then clamoring to get it back in an upright position. In his awkward attempt at doing so, he made an even more rattling noise.

Meanwhile Chalmer was already at the front of the room. He grabbed the man by the arm and jerked him around. "Hey, what do ya think you're doin'!"

"I'm spittin' in the bastard's face; that's what I'm doin'. I hated him and I'm glad he finally got what he deserved." His breath reeked with alcohol.

"Don't ya know there's a law against mutilatin' a corpse? I could arrest you for that." Chalmer didn't know whether that was true, but it sounded right and official too. It would make sense.

"Go ahead and arrest me. I'm just sorry I didn't have the guts to do it when he was alive--the no-good bastard." The man was shaking all over and stumbling, barely staying on his feet.

"Well, why don't ya take a seat over here and calm yourself down for a spell," Chalmer said, guiding him to the chair he had vacated. "What's your name and what's this all about."

"My name's Everett Manes, and that Pewzer, he stole my money."

"Stole your money? When was that?"

"About five years ago. I took a load of cattle to St. Louis to sell and had a pocketful of money when I got back. Pewzer, the dirty bastard, knew I liked the bottle and he acted like my old buddy and offered to buy me a whiskey. I couldn't pass up an offer like that, could I? Before I knew it, he got me drunk and I passed out. When I came to, my money was gone--all of it, and I was countin' on that money. It was about all I had to live on for the next several months." The man broke down in sobs, and tried to say more, but his slurred speech made it nearly impossible to make out what he was muttering.

"Well, why don't ya go on about your business and get out of here."

After he wobbled out the door, Chalmer and McIntire decided to call it an evening. "Let's get back to town and see if anything has come up there. I imagine Jenkins has already taken over the night shift, and we've got to get a little rest. I have to testify in court tomorrow morning--another domestic dispute, as usual. I don't know why some people don't know how to get along. I'll come back down here tomorrow afternoon--that is if court gets out early enough. The judges and lawyers don't get in any hurry, ya know. They just fiddle ass around and kill time, if they show up at all."

"Do ya want me to go along tomorrow? I'd sure like to," McIntire said.

"Suit yourself. There won't be much goin' on in Rothersby. Maybe you could pick up on somethin' I don't see."

McIntire stood a little taller at that remark. "Then I think I'll just go along. You can pick me up at the office when ya get finished in court."

When they drove into Struthersville the next day, Louella Pewzer was trying to sweet talk a man with a beaten up green pickup truck to haul Pewzer's casket out to the cemetery. She had paid a man to dig the grave. The drought-stricken ground was hard, and after digging four feet deep the grave digger had given up. "Well, what does it matter if he ain't six feet under?" he said when he reported back to Louella, who didn't care how deep the grave was.

The man with the truck resisted for a while, but finally succumbed to Louella's charms, swaying hips, and batting eyelashes. "Get me some help, and we'll load him up and then dump him out at the cemetery," he said.

After approaching a few of the town's dawdlers, Louella, again turning on the female charm, got four men to carry the casket out of Filber's store. They roughly hoisted it onto the back of the rusty pickup with a thud. "Hey, you guys, be careful there," the owner said. "You might damage my pickup." They all laughed, jumped aboard, and in unison, kicked the casket against the cab of the truck.

Chalmer and McIntire watched them head for the cemetery and heard Louella yell, "Just dump him in the grave and shove a little dirt over him."

Chapter 12

SNELLINGS, THE WHITTLER

Farther down Main Street, Chalmer spotted an old gray-haired, overall-clad whittler sitting on a wooden bench in front of the barber shop, a red and white barber pole to his left. He figured he might be a good one to get information from. He knew from his younger days that town whittlers didn't miss much of anything. "Hey there, old timer, ya mind if I sit here beside ya for a spell?"

The whittler answered without looking up and continued to shave bits of wood off a stick, letting the scraps fall to the sidewalk. His leathered, wrinkled hands working with precision, he carved nothing in particular--just spent his time whittling. "Don't mind atall."

"I'm Sheriff Chalmer and this is my deputy." McIntire remained standing.

"Pleased to meet ya. My name's Willard Snellings."

"How's it goin' today?"

"Oh, pretty good, I guess. Shore is awful quiet now that Pewzer's dead."

"Do ya mind if I ask ya some questions? We're tryin' to find out who wanted Pewzer dead and who did him in."

"Ask away, but I don't reckon I can tell ya much. They ain't nobody that's cryin' now that he's dead. I sure ain't. Why, one time I was settin' here mindin' my own business when he walks up and yanks my knife out of my hand and grabs my ear, and says, 'How would ya like to have this ear whittled off just like you're whittlin' that there stick?' I stared straight ahead and as steady as I could, I says, 'I wouldn't like it much.'

"He touched the knife to my ear. I felt a little blood trickle down, and then he says, 'Then how do ya think that there stick feels?' Then he let go of my ear and walked off laughin' a big horse laugh."

McIntire had a shocked, disgusted look on his face. "Golly durn, I don't guess ya wouldn't mind if we never could find his killer." He emphasized the word *we*, proud to be a part of solving the mystery. "If I was in your shoes, I shore wouldn't."

"Naw, whoever did it ought to get a big fat reward." With a shaky finger, he pointed to the door of the barber shop. "Why, one time Pewzer was in there gettin' a haircut, and the barber was trimmin' his side burns with a straight razor, and he grabbed it and threatened to cut that there barber's throat--only didn't, but not before he scared the shit out of him. And me too. I thought he was gonna do it shore 'nough." Just thinking about Pewzer and his meanness seemed to rattle the old man. "I seen lots of things out of Pewzer. If ya got a week or two, maybe I could tell ya about 'em, but mind ya, he didn't pick on ever'body. He knew who to leave alone. There's some people tougher than he was." He paused, then added, "Well, maybe just a few anyways."

"Well, we'd be glad to hear ya out--even if it does take a while. I need a suspect pretty bad, and this is the only case we've got right now. Actually, to be right honest about it, it's the only murder case I ever had."

The whittler thought a few seconds, and then with skepticism etched on his face, said, "But I reckon most of the people I know about wouldn't be able to kill him."

"But maybe they could've paid somebody to smash his head in," the sheriff suggested.

"Well, maybe some of 'em. But not all of 'em."

"Let me be the judge of that. I'd really appreciate any information you could give me." Chalmer withdrew a small notebook from his shirt pocket ready to jot down notes.

"Anyhow, it all started real bad after Opal and her kids left him. Before that, he didn't come to town all that regular. He had plenty of people to be mean to right there at home. I reckon after they left, he needed somebody to pick on, so he came to town real regular, and when people saw his old pickup comin', word got out that Pewzer was in town, and a lot of 'em scattered. But that didn't stop him from findin' somebody to pick on."

And so, the whittler gave Chalmer the first installment of the connection between the people of Struthersville and Ekbert Pewzer and the torment he left in his wake. The rest of the information Chalmer was able to fill in with subsequent interviews with some of Pewzer's victims, who were no longer afraid to talk now that Pewzer was dead and buried. It was time-consuming, but Chalmer had little else to do and just thinking of the glory he might receive if he solved a murder case like they always did on television made him determined to find the killer or killers. The detective shows on his new television set inspired him and prompted him to work hard at solving the mystery of Pewzer's death.

"And, by the way," the whittler said as Chalmer and his deputy turned to leave, "If ya want to learn a lot, Saturday's the time to do it. Ever'body comes to town on Saturday."

"They do? What for?" The sheriff asked.

"Oh, just to loaf. You know--to hang out and catch up on all the news. And buy their stuff of course."

Chapter 13

LAWRENCE PHILLIPS

Chalmer's first interview was conducted with the man who owned a well-stocked grocery and dry goods store. It was located on the opposite end of Main Street from Filber's. He and McIntire walked past a pot-bellied heating stove as they approached the owner.

"Boy, as hot as it is today, it's hard to believe that stove'll ever need to be used," McIntire said. To make it clear that he was to keep his mouth shut, Chalmer gave him a punch in the ribs with his elbow.

A mild-mannered, middle-aged man with a soft voice, Lawrence Phillips was obviously nervous as soon as Chalmer and his deputy walked into the store. He kept glancing at his somewhat dumpy, stringy haired wife, who was smiling and attempting to help a customer standing near the cash register. The little lady wanted to know where she could find the oregano.

"What's that?" McIntire muttered to Chalmer, who quickly elbowed him again, and out of the side of his mouth whispered disgustedly, "We're not here to shop!"

"If ya don't mind, we'd like to ask ya a few questions about any connections you might have had with Ekbert Pewzer," Chalmer said as they approached Phillips. Chalmer didn't miss how nervous he was. The whittler had told him about how strange it was that Pewzer had always taken whatever he wanted from the store and walked out laughing like he was rubbing it in when he instructed Phillips to put it on his bill. He figured Pewzer had something on Phillips but didn't know what it was. And now Chalmer intended to find out.

"We're investigating Ekbert Pewzer's death and thought you might be able to answer a few questions for us."

Phillips turned pale and fidgeted with some nearby canned goods, restacking them. "And what's that got to do with me?"

"Well, we hear tell he used to get his groceries here."

"So? Lots of people do. That's what I'm in business for."

"Did Pewzer pay for what he got?"

Just then, Phillips' wife finished ringing up a sale and walked toward them.

"Look, why don't we go outside. It's pretty hot in here," Phillips suggested, pulling at his collar. With the ceiling fan buzzing overhead, Chalmer figured it would be a lot cooler in the store than outside in the heat, but he sensed Phillips' discomfort with his wife waddling closer.

"Sure, whatever you say." It was obvious that Phillips didn't want to answer questions in the presence of his wife. They stepped outside into the humid air, and Chalmer waited until an elderly couple teetered by before firing off his question.

"I repeat, did Pewzer pay for what he got?"

"Why would you ask something like that?"

"Well, it seems that if he didn't pay for his groceries, he must have known somethin'. Maybe somethin' that ya don't want to talk about. I understand he always told ya to put it on his tab."

"So what? Lots of people do that, and they pay up, usually at the end of the month."

"Did Pewzer ever pay up, and have ya got any proof that he did? We checked his bank account and he didn't have any checks made out to you," Chalmer said with a straight face. McIntire coughed and cleared his throat knowing his boss had just told a lie.

Too quickly, Phillips said, "He always paid in cash."

Chalmer hesitated long enough to make Phillips even more uneasy and then told another lie, although convincing. "Ya know, Phillips, if we think you're lying, we can take ya in for impeding a murder investigation." He didn't know whether *impeding* was exactly the right word, but he was satisfied that it sounded important and legal enough.

Phillips took a handkerchief out of his hip pocket and began wiping at the sweat that had formed on his forehead. "I'll tell you whatever you want to know, but it's got to be strictly confidential. I don't want my wife to get wind of this, and I assure you I didn't have anything to do with Pewzer's murder if that's what you're thinking."

"We're listenin'," Chalmer said, and McIntire's snapped to attention. "What ya say won't go any farther--that is if ya don't become a viable suspect." Chalmer was proud of himself for using another big word. The crime shows he'd watched on television had reaped big rewards for this murder investigation.

Phillips voice dropped to a whisper, but he quickly related the event that led to Pewzer's taking what he wanted. He hesitated only when somebody came down the sidewalk. "Mind you, it was just a youthful indiscretion. I was kind of struck on this young woman who used to come in the store. She was a good-looking blonde and was always flashing those big . . . uh . . . those big titties of hers in front of me with her low blouses and all, and one day she asked if I'd take her for a ride that night in my new car. Well, how could I resist? I'm a man after all. To make a long story short, we parked up on this hill a little way out of town, and that's when Pewzer came by in his truck. He stopped and shined his flashlight in the car and asked if we needed any help, but he was laughing his ugly head off. We knew we were caught, and after that he never did pay a cent for his groceries. And I promise, I swear to God, I never did have anything to do with that woman again."

Chalmer didn't know why Phillips felt compelled to promise him any such thing, but McIntire was curious. "Who was the lady?"

Phillips looked at Chalmer. "Do I have to answer that?"

"It might not be a bad idea. I figure a woman could pay somebody to do Pewzer in as easy as a man could."

"If you ever find her, don't tell her I told you, but it was Gayla Cassidy. She's since moved away from here, and I don't know where. I guess she felt she had to. Pewzer kept threatening to tell the whole town if she didn't let him get in on the action and give him a little of that . . . that, you know . . . that pussy. I suppose it was easier for her to leave town than to do that. I just hope he didn't attack her. She used to live right up by the Baptist church." When Chalmer didn't ask anything else, he added. "Now, is it all right if I go back inside? I hope you don't think I did it. A few groceries wouldn't be worth killing somebody for, now would it?"

"If we have any more questions, we'll be in touch." The two strolled across the street, with Chalmer's head spinning with ideas. He remembered the bartender telling about seeing a light-headed woman talking to two men outside. It seemed he had another suspect, and he'd have to try to track this Gayla Cassidy down. Would the list never end, and how was he supposed to get to the bottom of this case with so many people who more than likely wanted Pewzer dead? But it was his sworn duty to try.

Eager to know what Chalmer was thinking, McIntire asked, "Do ya think he could've done it?"

"I suppose anybody could've done it. We've still got a lot of questions to ask of an awful lot of people." Chalmer looked up and down the street. "I guess we might as well go down to the blacksmith shop since we're this close."

Chapter 14

THE BLACKSMITH

A blast of hot air hit them the minute they sauntered into the blacksmith shop. A wiry little man with a red face stooped over the forge and seemed to be as tough as the metal he pounded on. The fire was hotter than Hades, and the rod the smitty was concentrating on and bending into shape glowed with a fiery red. A heavy, protective apron encircled his thin body. No one else was in the shop.

"Holy durn, he shore is a tough old geezer," McIntire whispered. "How does he stand it?"

The sheriff mopped his brow. "Used to it, I guess," Chalmer whispered back.

"Whew! How could anybody ever get used to that?"

They stood off to one side waiting for the blacksmith to finish bending the rod to his satisfaction.

McIntire shook his head with sweat pouring down his cheeks and answered his own question. "I don't reckon you'd ever get used to it. There ain't a breeze astirrin' anywheres."

"He's sure not the kind of blacksmiths ya see in picture books with their big muscled arms. He's as skinny as a rail."

After inspecting the rod and dipping into a vat of water to cool it, the smitty looked up, noticing the sheriff's badge. "What can I do for you gentlemen?"

"I'm Sheriff Chalmer and this is McIntire, my deputy. And your name is . . .?"

"Elijah Grant. Pleased to meet ya. What ya got on your mind?"

"We understand that you weren't any friend of Ekbert Pewzer, and we'd like to ask ya some questions--that is, if ya got the time."

"Shore thing, if it don't take too long. See that mare tied out there. I gotta fit a shoe for her and have her shod before the owner gets finished with his business."

"First off, tell us about any bad dealings ya had with him. We heard ya threatened him one time."

"I did for shore, and I'm proud of it. And you would've too considerin' the situation. But I didn't kill him if that's what you're gettin' at."

"We'd like to hear your side of the story if it's all the same to you."

"Well, he came in here one day struttin' his stuff like a big shot. I knowed we was in for trouble 'cause when he got like that, he was lookin' for somebody to beat around on. Kids are always hangin' around here. I like kids, ya know." He shook his head sadly. "I had a boy once but he was killed in a car wreck, just after my wife died. He had the biggest funeral down at the Methodist Church that was ever held in these parts." He paused as if picturing the funeral in his mind. "Anyway, the two Wasmer boys was watchin' me work on a horse shoe. They liked horses, ya know. Well, Pewzer came in here, and all of a sudden he grabbed my hot iron and stuck it in my face. Said he was gonna burn my eyeball out, but then he laughed and turned on the boys. They screamed and ran outside, but Pewzer chased 'em down and said he was gonna brand 'em right there on the spot. I started after him. I couldn't let him do any such thing. And then all of a sudden he yanked around and branded a horse right on the neck. She whinnied and bucked and kicked me down. I still got a bad limp from that there kick."

"Did he leave after that?"

"Yeah, but not before I told him I'd kill him if he ever came down here again. He laughed all the way up the street. After that I got a gun. It's right over there in the corner, and I'd have used it on him too. He was a mean son of a gun, and I'm glad he's dead, and so's ever'body that ever knowed him."

Convinced that the smitty could have killed Pewzer with a clear conscience, Chalmer asked, "You wouldn't have been the one that killed him, now would ya?"

"Naw, how could I do that? I hear he was killed at his house. I don't even own a car. How do ya think I'd get there? Beides, I tweren't no match for Pewzer. He was a lot bigger than me and a lot younger too."

"But maybe you could've paid somebody."

"Well, I would've liked to, but I didn't. Does that answer your question?" The smitty frowned, looking the sheriff straight in the eyes. "Ya got any more questions? I need to get back to work."

"That's all for now. Thanks for your time."

As they exited the shop and took a deep breath, McIntire conjectured, "I think I could've killed him if'n I'd witnessed all that. What do you think?"

"I'm not thinkin' anything. I'm just gatherin' evidence. Let's go talk to Snellings again."

McIntire looked confused. "Who?"

"You know, the whittler."

"Oh, yeah."

Snellings was still sitting on the bench, with shavings all around his feet, but this time he was using a whet rock to sharpen his knife. "You boys makin' any headway?"

"Not much," Chalmer said, "but I've got another question for ya."

"Ask away."

"Do ya know anything about Pewzer's first wife--the one that he had before Opal and her kids moved in with him? You wouldn't happen to know whatever happened to her, would ya?"

"Naw, I never heard anything about that." Not wanting to shout, the whittler waited for a train to rumble on down the tracks and whistle at the crossing before continuing. "That must have been before I moved here."

"Do ya know who might know somethin' about her?"

The whittler thought a few seconds and then said, "Well, if it was me, I'd check at the post office. They forwarded my mail here when I moved from Wheaton."

Coming over Chalmer was the recurring inferiority that had plagued him since childhood--the same one that had created his urge to run for sheriff. He had needed to feel important, and he thought sure that being sheriff would elevate his self-esteem. That inferior feeling had probably contributed to the breakup of his marriage to Sally eight months earlier. It seemed that soon after they were married, she was always nagging at him to think for himself. Now, he felt a little stupid. Why did an old whittler have to suggest the post office to him? He should have figured that out for himself.

Chapter 15

THE POST OFFICE

With McIntire trailing behind, Chalmer walked across a side street and stepped into the post office, where the white-haired postmaster, a rather handsome man for his age, stood on the other side of a partition that separated the patrons from the mail sorting. There was the strong odor of Lysol.

"I'm Sheriff Chalmer. It smells like you just gave this place a good sprayin'."

"Yeah, the Grimley's were just in here, and when they leave, I have to. They stink up the place pretty bad."

With his head held high, Chalmer said, "I'm investigatin' a murder, and I thought you might be able to help me locate somebody--maybe give me a forwarding address."

The tall, older man rubbed his clean-shaven chin and twisted his thin lips to one side. "Oh, that murder, huh? Well, we don't usually give out information about postal patrons to just anybody."

"I understand that, and I appreciate it that you're just doin' your duty in a conscientious way," Chalmer said, trying to soften him up a bit. He patted the badge displayed on his shirt. "But I'm not just anybody. I'm the sheriff."

"Well, I guess it'd be all right then, but I might not be able to help you any." He peered over the wire-framed glasses that perched on the end of his nose. "What do you need to know? Who is it you're looking for?"

"A Jolene Pewzer. I understand she lived around here a long time ago, and I thought she might've left a forwarding address."

"Well, sheriff, I've been here a long time, and the best I can recall, she came in here with her little boy and asked that her mail be forwarded to Cornwall. You probably know that's a little town two counties over."

Chalmer stuck out his hand for a firm handshake and thanked the postmaster. "You've got a great memory. You've helped a lot."

Chalmer and his deputy started to leave when the postmaster remembered something else. "Funny thing is she wanted her mail forwarded to Jolene Fairway. Can't say as I blame her for not wanting to use the Pewzer name. I know you feel obligated to investigate his murder. But nobody's sorry he's dead. Why, one time he grabbed a letter out of Alice Cellers' hand, just as she was getting it out of her box. It was a love letter from her boyfriend in the Army. He opened it up and went outside reading it loud enough for everybody to hear and making fun of everything he wrote. She was crying and begging him to give it back to her, and he just read that much louder. When he finished it, he threw it on the ground and walked off laughing like a hyena." The postmaster, who had been so tight-lipped a few moments earlier, had become quite loquacious, offering information he hadn't been asked for. He put his hand to his lips and shook his head. "You know, no mom or dad would let their little girls out of their sight when he was in town. They just didn't feel it was safe with all the things that had been told about him."

McIntire just stood with his mouth open, and Chalmer shook his head. "Oh, by the way, do ya happen to have a forwarding address for a Gayla Cassidy?" He thought maybe the postmaster with his good memory could give him some more information since he was suddenly in such a talkative mood.

"Let's see now." The postmaster searched through some papers. "Yeah, here it is. She moved out West--to Albuquerque, New Mexico.

If I recall right, she said her mother lived there." He jotted down the address and handed it to Chalmer.

Chalmer felt he really didn't need the address but thanked him again and said, "You've been a big help." He was relieved to know that Gayla Cassidy was no longer a suspect. It wouldn't make sense for her to plan a murder when she was that far away.

Without commenting further, the two men walked to their car. "Let's head back to town, the sheriff said. "I've about had all I can take of this place, especially in this heat. We'll take the weekend off and then start fresh Monday morning--maybe check on some phone numbers in Cornwall. We might be able to find this Jolene or her son." He squeezed his belly under the steering wheel. "On second thought, Monday might be a good time for you to hold down the fort at the office." He hoped that McIntire didn't detect that he was beginning to get on his nerves. Having somebody stick to him like bad adhesive tape didn't set very well with Chalmer--maybe another reason his marriage fell apart.

Back at his tiny efficiency apartment--no more than a hole in the wall with a living room, a galley kitchen, and a tiny bedroom and bathroom--the only one he could afford--Chalmer took a cold beer out of the refrigerator, plopped himself down on a ragged recliner, and mulled over all he'd learned about Pewzer. It seemed that just about anyone would have had reason enough to kill him or cook up a murder-for-hire scheme. But surely not everyone was intimidated by him. The whittler had as much said so. He'd have to ask the whittler more about that sometime.

He took the little notebook out of his shirt pocket and reviewed the first of his possible suspects. He felt sure it had to be somebody close to the victim, if a person could call the no-good Pewzer a victim. But who? In his gut, he was also convinced it had to be a paid job. There was Opal, as well as her kids, but they'd been out of the picture for years, so why now? It didn't make sense for them to have him killed after all this time. There were plenty of others, but whoever it was, they'd need the means to pay a pretty handsome fee to have a person killed. That wouldn't come cheap. Chalmer sighed and twiddled his thumbs. He decided to watch his favorite detective show that was just getting started on his snowy television set. Maybe he could get some usable information about solving a murder. Then he'd sleep on it that night.

Chapter 16

LOAFERS—THE HUMAN KIND

Sheriff Chalmer couldn't wait until Monday, however. On Saturday he decided to take the whittler's advice. It just might be a good day to smoke out some suspects. When he drove down Struthersville's Main Street, he understood what the whittler had meant. The town was abuzz with activity, the kind that was characteristic of many small towns on a Saturday. He scoured every nook and cranny in search of someone who could give him an idea of who the killer or killers might be.

Men, propping themselves up against the dismal buildings, lined the sidewalk on both sides of the street. Two young kids sat on the edge of the sidewalk licking ice cream from a cone heaped high with a double scoop. The boy licked and slurped on chocolate with the sweet stuff oozing down his chin, while the girl ran her tongue over strawberry. Chalmer figured they were brother and sister, but he noticed regretfully that another boy stood to the side begging his father for a nickel. He wanted an ice cream cone too, but the stingy father snapped, "What do ya think I'm made of anyway? Well, punk, it's sure not money!" Chalmer wanted to toss the kid a nickel but thought better of it. That may be the wrong move with an already belligerent father glaring at the kid. It's hard telling what he'd do.

A teenager across the street emptied a small packet of peanuts into a bottle of Coca-Cola and slurped on the cold treat, sucking out a mouthful of peanuts in the process. Afterward, he belched loudly enough for Chalmer to hear the noise that came from deep within the kid's gut. Chalmer just shook his head.

Through the door of the drug store, Chalmer noticed an eye-catching, well-dressed woman in a brightly flowered dress sitting with her legs crossed at the soda fountain. She propped her high-heels up on the rail, exposing the calves of her long legs and a bit of the skin above her knees. He went in to take a second look even though he knew she was too young for him--probably only thirty-five. His eyes flitted from her full breasts to her shiny red lips. The voluptuous brunette pivoted on the stool, her back erect, and caught him staring at her. She batted her eyelashes before locking her eyes on his. With a glass of Coke in her hand, she gave him a slow, seductive smile, licked her lips, and sipped her drink through a straw.

Chalmer's body heat rose several degrees, and his heart began to race so rapidly he feared it might jump out of his chest. He hoped nobody could hear it pounding. His gaze lingered on her, his emotions roiling within him, when he suddenly thought of his ex-wife. It sure didn't hurt to look, but he felt a tinge of guilt all the same. He wondered why this woman in her high-heeled shoes and red dress wasn't sitting in that little dress shop next door where most of the ladies gathered to gossip while their husbands did some gossiping of their own. But then again, Chalmer knew that men didn't gossip. They just got together to shoot the bull and collect the latest local scuttlebutt.

A red-headed, freckled face boy stood at the drug store's comic book stand, his head down, completely engrossed in the words and bright colors of a Superman comic book. From the back, a large man with gray hair, a double chin, and pot marks on his face, probably the druggist, quickly stomped toward the boy and roared, "Are you intended to pay for that comic?" His eyes pinched even closer to his hawkish nose.

The startled boy looked up and meekly answered, "No sir. I ain't got no money."

"Then get away from there!" he yelled, grabbing the boy by the arm and shoving him out the door. "And don't come back till you can pay for what you read!"

Chalmer felt sorry for the boy and was no longer interested in the lady at the soda fountain, but he wasn't here to check out woman. He was here to solve a murder case. He meandered down the sidewalk, to a gas station which was owned by Orville Swensen, a nearly bald guy who had just enough hair to be gray at the temples. "I see you're not too busy right now," Chalmer said as he approached the gaunt fellow with big ears that stuck out too far from his pint-sized head.

"Nope, shore ain't--ain't ever busy enough. What can I do for ya?"

"I was just wonderin' if ya ever had any trouble with Ekbert Pewzer."

"Well, one time when I was pumpin' gas in his truck, he just drove off and gas went ever' which way. He thought that was real funny and threw out his cigarette. I was lucky though. It didn't hit the gas, and I shore was relieved. I could've been blown all to hell."

"Nice guy, huh? What did ya do about him not payin' and drivin' off like that?"

"Well, sheriff, what would you do?"

"Nothin' I guess."

"And that's exactly what I done. Ever'body was scared to death of the bastard."

"Yeah, so I've heard." Chalmer heard a phone ring inside the small office. "Your phone's ringin'. You'd better get that."

"Naw, that's not my ring. Mine's two longs."

"Party line, huh? It must get pretty aggravatin' with everybody being able to listen in on your conversations."

"Nope, I don't see it that way. I never say anything that's all that private, and when I forget what somebody called me about, I just ring Ginny down at the central office, and she fills me in. She knows ever'thing, and it comes in pretty handy sometimes." Orville chuckled. "Besides, I get to listen to all the people on my party line, which ain't that many. Sometimes it gets right down entertainin'."

Just then a small man who could barely peer over the steering wheel of his black '48 Chevy pulled up to the pump, turned off the ignition, and with a booming voice that belied his size yelled, "Fill 'er up."

Chalmer crossed the dusty graveled street, and walked up the other side, questioning the male loafers as he went. One lazily picked his teeth with a homemade toothpick and then sucked at his teeth with gusto. Another pulled a harmonica out of his bibbed overall pocket and seemed to take pleasure in playing "Dixieland." No one seemed to notice. A feckless sort of fellow standing off to himself spit between the gap in his front teeth and barely missed an old woman passing by on the sidewalk. He wiped the edges of his mouth off with a disgustingly dirty hand.

A few men were bunched up together laughing and slapping their knees. One guy scratched his balls. Chalmer surmised that one of them had told a pretty entertaining joke. Only a dirty joke could get a response like that. An old man who appeared to have dementia didn't seem to catch on to the punch line. With a blank look that reflected his confusion, he looked at the others, saw that they were laughing, and then laughed also.

Off to himself, apparently lost in his own thoughts, another elderly gentleman rolled a cigarette, lit it, and drew a deep drag. He coughed and sputtered awhile before a man yelled, "Don't ya know them things are bad for ya!"

Suddenly, the men stood immobilized, and the banter came to a halt. A low-flying plane checking out a pipeline only a mile or so away droned overhead. All heads lifted, and eyes, squinting against the sun's rays, followed its path in the blue sky until it was out of sight. Like a switch had been turned back on, conversations continued as if they had never been interrupted.

Chalmer flicked ashes from his cigarette and asked each man the same question. "Do ya have any clue as to who might have killed Ekbert Pewzer?"

The answers were all pretty much the same:

"Nope."

"Sure don't."

"Who cares?"

"What difference does it make? He's already done in, ain't he!"

"Not a clue."

"Naw."

"How would I know?"

"You're the one that's supposed to have the answer to that."

Some just shook their heads, raised their eyebrows, or shrugged their shoulders to dismiss the question. Others remained motionless.

Chalmer marveled at this conspiracy of silence. Surely some of these men knew something, but if they did, they sure weren't telling it. Their lips were sealed--sealed as tight as a jar of canned fruit. Maybe they were just glad Pewzer was dead, no matter who did it. But maybe it'd be a better bet that a bunch of 'em got together and did the deed. He knew that mob violence could spur even decent men to action. When people get fed up and angry enough, and can't take it anymore, most anything can happen. Maybe just one or two tough guys beat him to death, but if anybody knew who did it, that's as far as it would go, and Chalmer was getting nowhere.

Like the whittler had said everybody comes to town on Saturday. He had definitely been right about that. It was anything but sleepy on this steaming hot day. It was an interesting experience, but the sheriff hadn't gained a thing by making a Saturday appearance. He wasn't one bit closer to solving Pewzer's murder, and a perfectly good Saturday had been wasted.

Chapter 17

SALLY, CHALMER'S EX-WIFE

That night was a restless one. Chalmer didn't dream about the case or the Saturday loafers in Struthersville. Instead, he dreamed about his ex-wife griping about how much time he spent at the office since he'd been elected sheriff. In the dream, he had made love to her in the house, in the bedroom, they had once shared--the one she now had sole possession of and the one he was still making payments on. Immediately, his dream changed to a nightmare and she was cheating on him. The perplexing dream disturbed him and left him with unanswered questions. It kept telling him that the divorce hadn't been all his fault. She had blamed him for everything, and he had paid for that blame with an overwhelming sense of guilt and sadness, and financial support. If it was partly Sally's fault, what had she done? Was his nightmare telling him something? His resentment grew, and he had to know.

The next morning, he realized he'd been so busy with Pewzer's murder that he hadn't had time to dwell on the divorce--a welcome reprieve. But now this dream was bearing down on him, and he was so groggy that he didn't feel he'd slept at all. He pushed himself off the bed, went to the bathroom, and splashed cold water on his face before sitting down to a breakfast of dry toast and stale coffee. He was still thinking of his dreams when he shaved and then cleaned up in the tiny cubicle called a shower. He could barely wedge his body into it.

He dressed in the same clothes he'd had on the day before and hoped they didn't smell too bad after the sweltering heat he'd been in. Maybe a double dose of roll-on deodorant would help. But for sure, he needed to take some clothes to the cleaners and visit a nearby Laundromat. He missed having someone to do that for him. Maybe he had depended on his ex too much. Sally had said often enough that she was his wife, not his mother or maid. He guessed she'd gotten tired of being his maid. He decided to go to the cleaners and the Laundromat on this lazy Sunday morning. Anyway, he wasn't due at the office until Monday. He almost wished he was compelled to go in for some kind of emergency. It would help him shake the nightmare that haunted him.

On Monday, Chalmer was relieved to see that McIntire wasn't there yet. The only available person was Jake Hobbs, who seemed to be content in his own world. Chalmer knew that the bushy eye-browed jailer listened a lot but talked very little. Hobbs always claimed to have big ears and a little mouth. Reluctant to ask him anything, Chalmer thought of the dreams he'd had and decided to take a chance. "Jake, could I ask ya somethin'?"

"Why, sure thing. You're my boss, ain't ya, and I appreciate the job. I'm beholden to ya."

"Well, you see, this is not about the job. It's about somethin' personal."

Hobbs was immediately interested, but his furrowed brow cast a bit of hesitancy in his demeanor. He didn't much like getting in on personal matters, but he said, "Okay. What ya got on your mind?"

Before explaining, Chalmer bit his lower lip and felt a bit guilty for involving Hobbs in his marital problems. "Well . . . uh, well, did you ever hear any rumors about my wife, my ex-wife, that is?"

"What kind of rumors?"

"Well, you know, maybe that she was runnin' around on me before she split."

"Do I have to answer that?"

"Naw, I don't suppose ya do, and I can't make ya, but I just gotta know, and who else am I gonna ask? I've been carryin' all this guilt around with me, thinkin' it was all my fault, and then I had a dream last night that got me to wonderin'."

Hobbs could sense Chalmer's distress by his tormented expression and was flattered that Chalmer would choose him to confide in. "Yeah, maybe there was somethin' to that dream of yours. I heard, now mind ya this is just hearsay, I heard she was runnin' around with some guy that lived way down by Dikerston--a married guy, I might add."

"How long ago was that? You mean when she was still married to me?"

"Yeah, for more than a year. But now don't quote me on that. You know how things get around."

"Did ya ever hear how she met him?" Chalmer struggled to suppress his anger. His dream had been accurate. She hadn't left him simply because of his many shortcomings as she had so often reminded him of. She had a far greater motive, and she'd blamed it on him--probably to assuage her own guilt. Through tired, squinted eyes and compressed lips, he waited for an answer.

"Well, let's see. Rumor has it that she got acquainted with him at some kind of political rally about the same time you were runnin' for sheriff."

"Do ya know his name?"

Just then McIntire strolled into the cramped office with his newspaper and a sack of donuts. Both men fell silent.

Chapter 18

JOLENE AND RICHARD FAIRWAY

Deciding that he needed to get in touch with Jolene Fairway, Pewzer's long-ago wife, Chalmer was back to the grind that morning and heading to Cornwall. He needed to stay busy. He was mad at the world, but it was good not to have that dumb-ass McIntire along. He needed a break from his stupid questions.

On the long drive, with his windows down and the hot air billowing in, he had plenty of time to reflect on what Hobbs had told him and on his now defunct marriage. He should have read the signs long ago, but he had been clueless. Maybe he didn't want to know anything. He recalled eating at the Daylight Cafe with Sally about a year ago and how the woman running the cash register had looked at him so pitifully. Her eyes had surreptitiously darted to Sally, trying to tell him something. Also he should have been able to read a message in her voice. He realized all that now and remembered similar incidents. But back then, he saw and heard only the things he wanted to see and hear.

Questions bombarded him. Was he less of a man than the guy Sally was making it with? What was it about himself that made him less desirable? He wished he knew. Sure, he'd gained a few pounds. But most middle-aged people had, and she had too. Well, not as much as he had, but neither one of them was getting any younger. Middle age didn't do much for anybody in the looks department. Maybe she was going through a mid-life crisis. He'd wanted kids, but she didn't--said it'd mess up her figure, like it was that good to start with. The more he thought about it, the angrier he became.

He was glad to know that at least it apparently wasn't all his fault. Maybe he'd have a chance to ask her about that sometime. He'd never wanted another woman, and even if he had, he would have stayed true to his marriage. It was a matter of principle. He didn't have a roaming eye, but apparently she did. And besides, no one could expect for a marriage to be smooth sailing all the time. Why did she? Give her time. She'd get tired of this other guy soon enough. Or maybe he'd get tired of her. Or maybe his wife would find out and give him an ultimatum--his mistress or her. He'd bet his life that Sally's lover would choose his wife. Divorces were messy, he well knew. The way he had to live now, with barely enough money to make ends meet after he paid court-ordered support to the bitch, was a disgrace. He predicted that she'd come begging back to him when the other guy dumped her. It'd serve her right. Then she'd see how it felt to get dumped like a piece of crap. His lips transformed themselves into a slow, steady smile, just thinking of that scenario, but that smile quickly turned to a frown. Maybe all that was just wishful thinking.

He was still engrossed in that thought when he realized he'd missed his turnoff. He pulled off to the side of the road and stopped to look at the road map in the seat beside him. It was hard to hold it in the right place with the wind blowing in the open window, but he finally located his whereabouts. Damn. He'd probably driven five miles or more out of his way.

Backtracking to the turnoff and driving several miles farther, he drove into Cornwall, a beleaguered town not much different from Struthersville. It seemed that all small towns were pretty much the same, only this one wasn't beside a railroad track. Now all he had to do was track down this Fairway man he'd located in the phonebook. Maybe he could direct him to Jolene.

Chalmer bought a buck's worth of gas at a service station that had one lone pump and asked the attendant--probably the owner--if he knew where Richard Fairway lived. Directed north about two miles out in the country, Chalmer was hopeful he'd find some answers. He needed to know as much about Pewzer's past as possible, and who might have wanted him dead. But he already knew too much. He knew that just about everybody who had known him could have killed him or had him killed for one reason or another.

A broad-shouldered man of about forty answered Chalmer's knock on the screen door of the ranch-style home. It was bigger and newer than those of most people Chalmer was acquainted with. The outside door was propped wide open to let in a slight breeze. Chalmer was surprised at how young the man seemed. He had figured that Richard Fairway was probably Jolene's brother. Two teenaged boys looked up from a table, where they were scooping food into their mouths.

"Who is it?" Chalmer heard a female voice ask.

Chalmer quickly introduced himself as the sheriff from Rothersby County. "And you must be Richard Fairway," he added.

"That's right. And what brings you way out here?"

"I thought maybe you could direct me to Jolene Fairway. Do you know where she lives?"

Fairway frowned. "And what would be your interest in her?"

"I understand she was married to Ekbert Pewzer for a while." Fairway turned pale and his hands began to shake, but once Chalmer had started, he wasn't about to be deterred. "Pewzer was murdered, and I'm trying to check out his background. I understand Jolene Fairway had a son by Pewzer." He hesitated to go on, but suddenly an epitome hit him. "You wouldn't happen to be that son, now would ya?"

Pewzer's Wake

The boys at the table, their bodies bolting with shock, nearly choked on their food and scrambled to Fairway's side with their expressions full of questions. So did the woman, his wife no doubt. They'd apparently read in the area-wide newspaper about Pewzer's murder and his alleged reputation.

Chalmer knew he'd hit spot-on when he saw Fairway's expression. He also knew his revelation was unwelcome news to both his wife and his boys, but he felt compelled to pursue the matter. "When did ya change your name?" Before giving Fairway a chance to answer, he continued with, "Now, mind ya, I wouldn't blame ya, but I need some answers if I'm gonna get to the bottom of this murder."

Fairway bristled and raised a belligerent fist, shaking it in Chalmer's face. His sons were just as hostile, only their anger seemed to be directed more at their dad. One yelled, "You mean that mean SOB is your dad and our grandfather! How could you do this to us!" He glared at Chalmer. "And how dare you come to our house and drop this bombshell on us!" He pointed an accusing finger at Chalmer and jabbed a finger in his chest, his anger escalating. He and his brother were completely out of control and were ready to take it out on anybody.

Chalmer didn't relish the thought of being beaten to smithereens. He was visibly shaken. He raised his hands, palm out, as if to defend himself and at the same time make peace. In an attempt to diffuse the situation, he said, "Now, boys, just calm down. Don't be mad at your dad. He can't help who his dad was any more than you can. Apparently he felt bad enough about it to take his mother's maiden name, or I suppose it was her maiden name. Ya ought to think about how he must've felt. I didn't mean any harm, honest I didn't. I didn't know that ya didn't know about . . . about . . . your roots."

Their anger gradually subsided and eventually turned to stunned disbelief. The son who was less vocal put in his two cents' worth, "Dad, you've got a lot of explaining to do. Do you remember this bastard Pewzer at all?"

"No. No, I don't. Just what Mom told me. He was mean to her after I was born, and according to her, he was mean to me too when I was not much more than a baby. And by the way, you need to watch your language."

"And that brings me to your mother again," Chalmer said, realizing that he probably wasn't going to have his face smashed in after all. "Where can I find her?"

"She's in a home in Ridgeway--a terrible place--but we couldn't keep her anymore. She's out of her mind." Fairway's voice trailed off. "I feel guilty every time I think about it or whenever I go see her. She did the best she could for me, and I love her, or at least love the person she used to be."

Aware that Jolene Fairway or her son could no longer be a suspect because they had tried to erase Pewzer from their memory years earlier. Realizing they couldn't even furnish any new information, Chalmer regretted the turmoil he'd caused this family. He knew from the beginning that it was a long shot anyway. All he could do was apologize and leave, wondering what would transpire in that household after he was gone. That bothered him all the way back to Rothersby. At least, it took his mind off his own problems about Sally.

Chapter 19

SURPRISES

For the next few days, Chalmer took care of a bunch of little things, as he called them. The usual stuff had been piling up on his desk. There were several complaints about noisy neighbors or something that wasn't handled to people's satisfaction. It would be safe to ignore most of those. Some were complaints about somebody's cow getting in the wrong pasture or hogs rooting up a garden or something similar--things that had long since been resolved in one way or another. People just had to get their disgruntled gripes off their chests, and where better to do that than at the sheriff's office? In time they'd simmer down, and that would be the end of that.

He had another summons to appear in court, and there was a letter requesting information from a law enforcement official in another county. He'd get right on the important things, but most of them he tossed in the over-flowing wastebasket under his desk.

He felt a need to get back to Struthersville, but he needed to put Pewzer's murder aside for a while and clear his head. On those television shows, the cops always seemed to solve things better when they had their minds on something else--when they were relaxing a bit. Things just suddenly came to them, and the case was solved. He hoped it would be that easy for him; however, in his gut, he knew his case wouldn't be that simple. His case wasn't a television show where everything just fell into place. It would take some real detective work.

Anyway, he needed the rest, and on one of those days he needed to buy a birthday cake for McIntire and invite the other men who served in his office. He wanted it to be a surprise. And it sure enough was when McIntire walked into the office after getting a bite to eat for lunch. "Happy birthday," they all shouted, pleased to see the look of shock on his face as they bunched up together and squeezed their bodies against the wall in the tiny office.

"How'd ya know it was my birthday? I never told nobody," McIntire said.

"Well, we're not a bunch of dummies," Hobbs said. "The sheriff here looked on the application ya filled out when ya applied for the job, but he had a pretty good idea anyhow. He keeps a record of them things in that little book he keeps in his shirt pocket."

Chalmer got out his lighter and lit the nineteen candles on the cake that said, "Happy Birthday, James." He had bought the cake at the town's only bakery.

"Blow 'em out," Jenkins said, and McIntire did just that with some help from Jenkins.

Chalmer could tell McIntire was embarrassed when a tear trickled down his cheek, which he quickly brushed aside with a shaky finger. "I don't ever remember havin' a real birthday cake before--not one just for me anyhow," he said, reflecting on how his birthday fell close to his dad's.

"Oh, I forgot to bring a knife," Chalmer said, frustrated at his lack of foresight, but he laughed it off. He admitted to himself that men weren't good at things like that. Anyhow, that's what women were for. They always took care of things like that, and he didn't think like a woman.

Jenkins reluctantly got out his big pocket knife, flipped it open, and cut the cake, thankful that it was just a single layer. McIntire discovered that it was a dark chocolate, his favorite. It was a messy affair when they all ate a big gooey piece of cake right out of their hands. Chalmer thought his sticky desk would never be the same, but he was glad that McIntire had been so pleased. After all, he was a good kid, sometimes annoying, but he meant well.

However, the real surprise--a much bigger one--occurred later that day. In walked a man who was almost a mirror image of Chalmer. His hair was also thinning, and he had a nose that was probably too big for the rest of his face. He first looked at Chalmer and then eyed McIntire, the only other person in the office, with apprehension clouding his face. "Can we go some place private to talk--some place *real* private?" he asked Chalmer, who was both curious and wary of this man who looked so much like himself. He wasn't quite sure he wanted to be alone with him. Maybe he had some vendetta against him or hated the law in general, but shouldn't a sheriff be brave enough to confront any situation that presented itself? He didn't want to act like a coward. Besides, curiosity overrode his wariness. Who was this man, and what did he want? But then again, he must have crossed paths with this guy sometime in the past. He had to know when and where.

"Sure. Let me get my hat," the sheriff said with bravado as he grabbed the brimmed hat that matched his tan uniform. Then he turned to McIntire. "You're in charge until Jenkins comes back in. We'll be at my apartment." He wanted to make sure somebody knew where he was--just in case something bad happened to him.

Reluctantly, Chalmer drove the man to his ground-floor, tan-bricked apartment that was just a few steps from the sidewalk. The rectangular structure had been hastily and poorly constructed after World War II. Small air-conditioners protruded from all the windows on the front side of the building. He thought briefly that he might be deranged for bringing a stranger he knew nothing about to his apartment, but he couldn't shake the eerie feeling that he ought to know this man who resembled himself.

He unlocked the door and flipped on the window air conditioning unit before the two exchanged any words. He suddenly became aware of how desolate and nondescript his apartment must look to a stranger. There were no neatly framed pictures of family members. In fact, there were no pictures at all to adorn the bare walls. The only picture he possessed was the wedding picture of him and Sally which he carried in his wallet.

"My name's Josh Chalmer," the man finally said after his eyes had lazily taken in the lack of decor. "A few days ago I saw in the Springfield paper where a Rothersby sheriff named LeRoy Chalmer was in charge of a murder investigation. I thought it was probably a long shot that it might be my long-lost brother, but I decided to find out. I couldn't live with myself if I didn't. Then when I walked in your office and saw you, I knew I had hit pay dirt."

The sheriff had a difficult time letting all this soak into his turbulent mind, and he was in turmoil with questions exploding like fireworks. He felt himself collapsing inside. He remembered having an older brother named Josh in an orphanage, but that was a long time ago and he had tried to push all that out of his mind. He had cried when he was put in foster care and Josh had been left behind. Josh had protected and comforted him for a very long time. They had been inseparable, even if they were in an orphanage. And now he didn't know what to say when after all these years they met again. He had to do something, so he stuck out his hand for a handshake with his newly found brother.

But shaking hands wasn't enough for Josh. He grabbed Chalmer and gave him a big bear hug. "Well, aren't you glad to see me?" Josh asked.

"Why sure. It's just such a shock, that's all."

"I didn't figure your name would still be Chalmer. I figured the people that adopted you would give you their name."

"Uh, well, they never did actually adopt me. I guess they didn't want to give up the money they got for bein' foster parents."

"Well, of all things. I never heard the like."

"Ya know I cried for ya every night after they took me away from ya."

"Yeah, I know what you mean. I cried for you too, but I wasn't about to let anybody know it. I'd just cover up my head at night and stifle the sobs. I was tough, you know. I had to be. But I couldn't help remembering how you cried, wanting Mommy when we were first dumped, and I needed to know if you were all right after they took you away. That bothered me a lot, really haunts me to this day."

In his mind, LeRoy speculated about how the nuns must have beaten good English and proper enunciation into Josh during the years he was there. Maybe he could have used some of that himself.

After an awkward silence, the sheriff asked, "Are ya hungry?"

"You bet."

"I could fry us up some eggs and make some toast. That's about all I got."

"Sounds good to me."

While they ate their eggs in the narrow kitchen that was hardly more than a hallway, Josh became silent as if something was bothering him. He finally pulled out a piece of paper and handed it to the sheriff. "I think you'd better see this."

"What is it?'

"Open it up," Josh said in a low voice.

Upon unfolding the paper, Chalmer saw that it was a wanted poster. He let his jaw drop, and his eyebrows curled in disbelief. "Oh!"

"Yeah, that's how I thought you'd react."

"You're a fugitive from the law!" The staggering impact of what he was reading nearly overwhelmed him.

"Yeah, we sure went different directions, didn't we?"

"What'd ya do?" The sheriff wasn't sure he wanted to know, but he asked the question anyway.

"A guy in a beer joint called me a mother . . . uh . . . you know, and I didn't like that much. I lost my temper--actually lost all control--and beat him nearly to death . . . or I guess he's still alive, but I didn't stay around to find out. I do know he was in the hospital for a long time. Anyway, I guess that makes me a fugitive from the law, and I know that makes it bad for you with you being an officer of the law and all."

Uncomfortable discussing this with his brother, the sheriff said, "Ya always did have a hot temper. Ya need to watch that."

"I know that, but when it's born and bred in ya, it's hard. I learned in that orphanage not to take any crap off anybody--not even from the nuns that tried to keep me in line."

"Then I guess you were never put in foster care?"

"Naw. Who'd want me? But I left that place as soon as I turned seventeen."

The sheriff fingered the wanted poster, his eyes squinting with displeasure and his mouth dry. His tongue felt too big. "Where'd ya get this poster?"

"Tore it off a post office wall, that's what I did."

The sheriff didn't want to hear more, didn't want to be involved. Eager to change the subject, he asked, "Do ya know why our folks dumped us in the orphanage in the first place?"

"No, don't know, and don't care. But it's pretty obvious that they didn't want us."

"Or couldn't take care of us. Maybe our dad took off to parts unknown, and our mother couldn't raise us."

"From what I can tell, we were just the first ones to get dumped by our so-called mother."

Chalmer's head drew back, his eyes snapped, and he grasped for words. "What do ya mean--the first ones? Ya mean there were others!"

"Yeah, that's what I mean."

"Explain yourself, man!"

"Well, you know how I was always sneaking around spying on the nuns?"

"Yeah, yeah. Go on."

"Well, it seems a baby girl was dropped off on the steps of the orphanage. She had a note pinned to her that said Iris Chalmer. The nun was disgusted. No, she was madder than a hornet. She said something about another one of those Chalmer brats and when's she gonna quit popping out kids for us to take care of."

"You're sayin' we got a sister out there somewhere?"

"That's what I'm saying, but that's long past. She wasn't at the orphanage long. Some couple adopted her. You know a sweet little baby girl is a lot more desirable than two ornery boys. But it doesn't matter a whit to me one way or the other." He studied his hands for a few seconds and asked, "Did you ever get married? This apartment doesn't look like it's made for two."

"I got married all right, but she divorced me several months ago, and believe me, I got bamboozled in the bargain."

"You mean she got the best end of the bargain?"

"She sure did." The sheriff got out his pack of Marlboros. "Want one?" he asked.

Josh shook his head. "I don't smoke."

"Good for you. It's an expensive habit," he said as he lit up.

"What about kids? Did you ever have any?"

Naw, none. I wanted them, but Sally--she's my ex--thought she was too good to have kid--said it'd be bad for her figure. What about you? Did you ever get married?"

Josh chuckled in a whimsical, self-deprecating way. "Now what woman would want me?" He acted as if he thought the answer to that question was obvious. He put his index finger to his lips, momentarily lost in thought. "What happened to your foster parents? Do they live around here?"

"Both dead."

"Oh, I'm sorry."

"Don't be. Anyway, they never had much to do with me after I was all grown up and didn't provide any income for 'em anymore."

The two brothers sporadically watched television and in between scenes reminisced about their time together in the orphanage. They also caught up on other parts of their lives. Well after midnight, Chalmer tossed Josh a sheet and blanket, the only spare ones he had, and told him he could sleep on the couch.

That night Chalmer dreamed of being kicked out of office for harboring a fugitive from the law and not turning his brother in. He woke up in a cold sweat, kicked the sheet aside, and sat up in bed. Burying his head in his hands, he was having a disturbing struggle with his conscience. He was sworn to uphold the law, but it just didn't seem right that the long arm of the law should be long enough for him to turn in his long-lost brother. After tossing and fighting the sheets for a very long time, he finally dozed off until his alarm went off the next morning.

When he awoke and stumbled into the living area, the sofa was empty with the sheet and blanket folded neatly. His brother had solved his dilemma for him, but a deep, unsettling sadness nearly overcame him. Josh was gone--lost as if he'd never been found. He had many questions he wanted--no needed--to ask the big brother that he had once looked up to, depended upon, and mourned for. He wondered if other wanted posters bearing a picture that looked remarkably like himself might someday be staring him in the face. He lit a cigarette and made some coffee. In his mind he conceded that it was better that Josh had moved on, but the troubling thing was he would have a difficult time moving past this dramatic surprise, and it left him in a quandary that he didn't want to deal with now or in the future.

"Who was that guy that came in here yesterday," McIntire asked as soon as Chalmer appeared back at his office. "What'd he want? He shore acted like it was secret and all, and he shore looked a lot like you."

"Now that's not any of your business, is it?" Chalmer snarled, unable to explain the visitor to himself, much less to somebody else--especially not to a young punk who was still wet behind the ears.

Chapter 20

BACK TO STRUTHERSVILLE

"Can I go along? Huh? Can I?" McIntire asked on Sunday morning when Chalmer announced that he'd decided to get back down to Struthersville to question some more people--that he'd have better luck finding people at home on a Sunday afternoon. When Chalmer didn't respond, McIntire explained himself. "I need to see how an expert does things. I can shore learn a lot from you."

The flattery worked. "Oh, come on, but I'd think you'd get tired of that stinkin' little burg. I know I sure am."

The town was nearly deserted when they arrived there, but the parking lots of the two churches were full to capacity. The whittler, wearing his customary overalls, apparently didn't attend church because there he was, sitting in his usual spot on the bench in front of the barbershop, just whittling away. Chalmer, not a churchgoer himself, thought Snellings wouldn't be very welcome in church with his faded, tattered overalls, especially when everyone else would be dressed up in their Sunday-go-to meeting best. "Howdy," Snellings said when he saw the two men approach.

"Howdy yourself. Boy, there's not much action around here--just a few hangin' out. Just about everybody must go to church on Sunday. I take it this is a pretty religious town."

"Yeah, I guess ya could say that. At least on Sunday anyhow. Maybe that's the only day." The whittler smiled. "Over at the Baptist

79

church, I hear tell, they keep a pretty tight rein on the kids--or maybe try to. Especially one old lady. Her name's Miss Finestein. One day a few of the kids was laughin' about it and claimed she tries to be their conscience and sends 'em on a guilt trip if they get out of line."

"What do ya mean?"

"Well, she tells 'em how bad it is to dance and do all kinds of things. You know, the things kids like to do. She even tells some of 'em that God's callin' 'em to preach."

"Wow, I'd say that's some kind of woman."

"I guess she's a good woman--just wants ever'body to live the way she does. I guess she does all that 'cause she really cares about 'em." Momentarily, he fell silent, wistful almost, before continuing. "Nobody ever cared that much about me when I was a kid--still don't."

Puzzled by the personal comments of the whittler, who never talked about himself--only about other people--Chalmer said, "But look at you. You sure turned out all right. You're always good to everybody, and you've been a lot of help to me." However, he was curious about Snellings' life--how he had grown up with nobody caring about him, with no family now or in the discernible future. It was the first time he had really seen the whittler with a heart and soul--with longings, regrets, and hopes like everybody else.

Snellings whittled awhile before changing the subject and focusing on something else. "I see you're still working on your murder case. Any progress yet?"

"Nope, none whatsoever. In fact, it gets harder all the time, with so many of Pewzer's enemies comin' to the surface. You'd think religious people wouldn't have so much hate in 'em, but I suppose if he was as bad as they say, it'd be hard to forgive him." Chalmer cupped his chin, turned his head to one side, and squeezed his lips together. He was thinking about the whittler telling him that not everybody was scared out of their wits by Pewzer. "By the way, I'm just curious. Who wasn't scared of him or at least not intimidated by him?"

Snellings spit on the sidewalk to his right. "Well, there was the Barnhart boys. They're big strappin' fellas that nobody messes with--not even Pewzer. They live out of town on a big family farm and just come in to buy stuff at the feed store and maybe a few groceries. Naw, Pewzer knew better than to pick on them. But they sure didn't mind botherin' Pewzer. Why, one time Pewzer was pesterin' Burk and Lyle and them big ol' boys took care of that problem."

"Who's Burk and Lyle, and what was Pewzer doin'?"

"Their last name's Tuebner, and well, I don't know quite how to say it, but they're real poor and real old--probably live on a old-age pension--and they ain't too smart. Lyle is deaf and Burk sort of takes care of him when he comes to town." He pronounced the word *deaf* with a long *e*. "Once ever' little whip snitch, Burk gets some baloney and crackers at the store across the street and sticks it in his hip pocket. Well, one day Pewzer grabbed the baloney out of his pocket and dared him to come get it. When Burk made a stab at gettin' it, he threw it on the ground along with a bunch of pennies. Lyle saw the money hit the ground and he got on his hands and knees and started scramblin' for it, feelin' around like crazy to get ever' last one of 'em. Well, you can imagine that was a hoot for Pewzer. He was laughin' and havin' a whale of a time."

The whittler paused, grinned just enough to show his rotten snags, and then drawled, "But he picked the wrong time 'cause just then the Barnhart boys drove into town. They didn't take to nobody doin' that, and they grabbed Pewzer up by the neck and made him pick up the baloney and the pennies and give 'em to the two old fellas. They made him apologize too. He shore didn't laugh anymore, at least, not that day. He just tucked his tail, jumped in his pickup, and left town. The Barnharts told Burk and Lyle to let 'em know if Pewzer ever bothered 'em again. And I reckon he didn't, least ways that I ever seen, and I don't miss much."

Chalmer knew that was true. He thanked Snellings for the information and said, "I guess as soon as church is out, we'll try to catch this Agnes Gilbert that you told us a little about the other day."

The whittler's eyes grew wide and he cocked his head to one side. "Oh, I don't think there's any need to wait till church is out. After what happened to her, I hear tell she's too ashamed to go to church."

"That bad, huh?"

"Yep, sure is. But I don't see any reason for ya to ask her any questions. I shore don't think she coulda been your killer. She's just a puny little woman and gettin' up there in years."

"Let me be the judge of that, okay?"

"Then, don't tell her that I'm the one that mentioned her name."

"Sure thing. We appreciate all your help, and what you tell us is strictly confidential, right McIntire?" McIntire nodded in agreement.

Chapter 21

THE WIDOW

As they drove down a dead end street and spotted the right address, Chalmer told McIntire to stay in the car while he asked Agnes Gilbert some questions. He thought she might be more reluctant to answer his questions with two men standing there listening to everything she said.

But he needn't to have been concerned because when she wobbled to the door and saw the sheriff's badge, the short, gray-haired woman with pale, withered cheeks and a double chin almost went into a panic and said, "I've not got anything to say to you or anybody else."

"I just wanted to ask ya a question or two about Ekbert Pewzer, that is, if ya don't mind."

"Well, I do mind!" She shook her head, waddling the skin that sagged under her chin, and glared at the sheriff. Battling back tears, she flatly refused to answer any questions about Pewzer before slamming the door to her white frame house in Chalmer's face, almost clipping his nose.

That left Chalmer with only one option. He'd have to go back to Snellings and coax him into telling what he had heard about the connection between Agnes Gilbert and Pewzer. It was now more of a curiosity that drove him to pursue answers about her than it was his investigation. He didn't see how she would be capable of harming anyone. A little dried-up woman with a limited income

Helen Breedlove

would be incapable of murder or a murder-for-hire even if she had reason enough to, and from the look on her face, she apparently had plenty of reason.

The whittler was glad to accommodate Chalmer and field his questions. "Ya know how Pewzer had a mean streak that'd stretched all the way from here to the next county. Well, Agnes had been a widow woman for about a year, and I hear tell, she was pretty lonesome. She ain't the best lookin' woman ya ever seen. In fact, some people would say she's right down ugly and the chances of her gettin' another man was pretty nigh impossible, to say the least. Pewzer knew that, and I reckon he thought he'd have some fun out of it."

The whittler momentarily stopped shaving his stick and looked up. "Now mind ya, this is all hearsay, and if anybody asks, ya didn't hear it from me. Anyways, he let on like he was comin' courtin' and bought her a box of chocolates. She was real thrilled and all. But the thing is, he'd put Ex-Lax inside some of the chocolates--the dirty scoundrel. She ate a lot of 'em and that made her real sick. You know how that is, with the trots and all. But he acted like he didn't have nothin' to do with the way she was sick and took her some flowers for a get-well present. She took one whiff of the flowers and startin' sneezin' and coughin' somethin' terrible. He'd put pepper or somethin' in the flowers. Well, that . . . er . . . caused an accident in her pants, and he laughed so hard he nearly doubled over. She ain't hardly showed her face in town since--only when she needs to get her mail once a week and maybe get a few groceries."

At that moment, Chalmer thought he'd like to have been the one that killed Pewzer. What a thing to do to a poor innocent widow woman! No wonder she didn't want to talk to him about Pewzer. She was too ashamed to, and he didn't blame her one little bit, but all he said was, "Why, that dirty bastard!" McIntire didn't say anything. He was too flabbergasted.

Snellings rubbed his whiskered chin and resumed his whittling in silence.

After a few minutes, Chalmer, realizing that the whittler was finished talking, thanked him and told McIntire he thought he'd go talk to Mary Davis, Louella's half-sister. If she was as sick as Louella had let on, she surely wouldn't be in church. Louella had told him Mary had some kind of debilitating nerve disease, but didn't say exactly what it was.

Chapter 22

MARY DAVIS

When Mary Davis answered the door, Chalmer couldn't help noticing that she seemed groggy and half dazed. She had trouble standing, and her speech was slurred. "I'm Sheriff Chalmer, ma'am, and I'd like to ask ya a few questions if it wouldn't be too much trouble. I hope we didn't wake ya up."

"I know who you are," she muttered. "And you didn't wake me up. I'm just lethargic today."

Confused as usual, McIntire said, "Le...what?"

She pressed a hand to her head. "Lethargic, you know tired and sleepy. I've not been feeling very well lately."

McIntire couldn't understand why people had to use such big words, and he wondered where Mary had learned them. Why couldn't people just use plain old English?

Chalmer punched McIntire in the ribs, giving him a warning to keep his stupid mouth shut. "I'm sorry to hear that, ma'am. Louella said you'd been a mite puny." He regretted calling her problem a *mite puny* as soon as he said it. He knew it was much more than that. "Do ya feel up to answerin' a few questions?"

Unsteadily hanging on to the house's tan siding, she stepped out on the porch to let herself down on a small porch swing. Chalmer thought for a second that she was going to miss the seat entirely and fall. He moved closer and was ready to grab her, but holding on to the side of the swing, she made contact with the seat on her own.

She breathed heavily as if gasping for air. "I guess so, if it wouldn't take too long." She seemed completely unfocused and murmured, "Louella takes good care of me."

"Well, that's good of her. She seems to be a fine person." Cautious and now quite leery about questioning this sick woman, he wiped sweat from his forehead before saying, "I reckon you know I'm tryin' to track down Ekbert Pewzer's killer." Almost apologetically Chalmer added, "It's my sworn duty, ya know." He thought how sometimes the long arm of the law reached into places it probably didn't have any business reaching into, but like he'd said, it was his duty.

Expressionless, as if numb to the world, Mary looked up and in a barely audible monotone voice asked, "And what's that got to do with me?"

"I thought ya might have heard somebody threaten to kill him or knew of somebody that'd like to see him dead. I understand ya lived at his house for a long time."

"Yes, regrettably I did, and to be right honest about it, that'd be anybody that ever had any dealings with him." Exhausted from fatigue and with her hands quivering, she said, "Including me. Now can I go back inside? I feel like I need to go lie down awhile."

Chalmer had already heard how Pewzer had molested her when she was just a young girl. Being aware of all Pewzer had done riled the hate in him. "Could ya answer just a few more questions? Then we'll leave ya alone."

"Maybe." She released a huff of breath and seemed relieved that the interview was about over.

"Can you tell me where we could find your oldest brother? We've not been able to locate him yet."

"If you're thinking Billy's a killer, you're wrong. He couldn't have done it."

"How's that?'

Mary stared straight ahead as if she didn't plan to answer Chalmer's question. Then abruptly she mumbled, "He's in prison . . . has been since April."

"Oh? What'd he do?"

"He robbed a gas station." Her voice grew weaker. "He was just trying to survive the best he could since he ran away from home, if you could call it that."

"Do any of you ever go see him?"

"Not me. I don't feel up to it, but Alvin and Louella do. And Mom too. I'm glad they're able to show him that somebody still loves him. I know I sure do." Mary took a shallow breath, her voice trailing off to almost a whisper. "If you understand someone's background and where they're coming from, it's easy to forgive them--to pretty much hold them blameless for anything. That bastard Ekbert Pewzer messed him up real good." She looked away sorrowfully, just staring into space. "Now can I go in? I feel like I'm about to pass out."

"Sure can. Thanks for your help. And I hope ya get to feelin' better." He was afraid she might faint right on the spot. He helped her off the swing and opened the screen door for her. "Can ya make it to the bed by yourself?" he asked.

She nodded and eased herself inside the house, holding onto anything she could grasp.

As he walked back to the car, Chalmer figured one likely suspect had been eliminated. A guy in prison couldn't very well commit murder. But later he had second thoughts. Or could he? Maybe he could have hired somebody, but who and with what? If he was so poor he had to resort to robbing filling stations, where would he get the money to pay someone? Other questions nagged at him. Why would Louella and Alvin and their mother say they didn't know where he was? Or had they simply said, "I can't say"? There was a subtle difference in *not knowing* and *not saying*. Maybe they were too ashamed to admit he was in prison, or then again, just maybe it could be something else entirely. He'd have to mull that over for quite a spell.

But right now, he just wanted to get back to town and finish a private conversation with Jake Hobbs. He needed to know the name of the guy his ex was getting it on with even before the divorce. The more he thought about it, the more bitter he became, and the more determined he was to find out. In the meantime, it was a relief to know that he wasn't entirely culpable for the divorce as Sally's accusatory remarks had so often reminded him. Up to this point, his ex had him convinced that everything was his fault in one way or the other. He'd have to try to catch Hobbs alone another time to learn more about this guy she was seeing all along.

That opportunity presented itself sooner than he would have expected when he stepped into his office earlier than usual the next morning. Back in the cell area, Hobbs was fixing breakfast for the few men still incarcerated. "Hobbs, as soon as you're finished there, come into my office. I'd like to ask ya somethin'."

"Sure thing, boss."

A few minutes later, Hobbs settled himself into the only spare chair in the office.

"What ya need to know?" he asked, but he already had a good idea what Chalmer's question would be.

"Do ya know the name of that fella you were tellin' me about--you know, the one that was runnin' around with my wife?"

"Well, I hear it was maybe a local politician over in the Gowson county seat. I think his name's George Trowler."

Without saying a word, Chalmer banged his fist on the desk and jumped up. "If anybody needs me, call me on the car radio. I think I'll take a look-see over that way."

At that moment, the door opened and then slammed shut. McIntire walked in. "Where we goin'? Are we goin' back to Struthersville?"

"*We're* not goin' anywhere. I'm goin' by myself, and I don't need you along. This is private," Chalmer snapped.

"Oh . . . . Shucks, I just thought . . ."

"That's your trouble. You think too much, and you know what? It gets pretty tiresome."

McIntire knew it was time to clam up. "Then I guess I'll just take care of things here."

"Good idea."

Chapter 23

LOVER BOY

When Chalmer entered Dikerston, the county seat of Gowson, he felt a bit guilty for driving his sheriff's car for personal business, not that anybody would care. And hell, it was the only car he *could* drive now that his ex-wife had the car he'd owned with her. Since the split, she had it, and it griped him to no end that he was still making payments on it. As he'd told his brother, he sure got bamboozled.

He parallel parked along the sidewalk and decided to sit there and wait and see what he could find out. It was hotter than hell and he was madder than hell too. He'd just sweat it out. He hoped he didn't have to piddle-ass around this town for long, but he wanted to know what this lover-boy George Trowler looked like.

Fortunately, he didn't have to wait long. As sweat poured off his face, he heard somebody say, "Hello, Mr. Trowler. How are you today?" The voice came from a sixty-something female. Chalmer ducked down but peered over the steering wheel.

Like a true politician, George Trowler answered in a smooth, patronizing manner. "Well fine, Mrs. Callaway. I see you're looking just as lovely as usual, even on this hot day." Mrs. Callaway covered her mouth with both hands, giggled like a school girl, and walked on down the sidewalk, probably unaware that Trowler was congratulating himself for another easy vote in the next election.

Chalmer thought he would gag, but at least, he now knew what he was up against. With his chest puffed out, Trowler's tall frame stood erect, and he brushed a thick crop of black hair away from his forehead. His self-importance was obvious, sickeningly obvious, as he strutted like a proud peacock into a nearby cafe. Chalmer knew right then that Trowler was just using his ex. She wasn't all that much of a catch. He probably had lots of women on the side. He knew, too, that his own looks and demeanor couldn't begin to measure up to this slick politician.

Chalmer got out of his car and walked inside the cafe, relieved that the air conditioning was doing its job. As he stood just inside the door, not sure that he wanted to go through with his plan, he spotted Trowler sitting in a red booth drinking coffee, of all things, on this hot day. The cafe had only a few other customers. Chalmer watched a couple of old men roll their own cigarettes--one using tobacco out of a can of Prince Albert and the other out of a small pouch, which he pulled shut with a string using his teeth. The guy ran his tongue across the paper to seal the cigarette. Chalmer was glad he carried a pack of Marlboros. But he wasn't here to smoke; he was here to smoke out the guy who was having an affair with his wife--now, thanks to this guy, his ex-wife.

Holding hands and gazing longingly into each other's eyes, a young couple sat across from each other in a booth. From the jukebox came the sounds of "Love Is a Many-Splendored Thing." Chalmer remembered regretfully when he and Sally felt that way about each other. Yeah, sure, love was a many-splendored thing when it went your way. When it didn't, it was shit, pure and simple. He was bitterly mad at the world, and he didn't want to see anybody who was halfway happy. It somehow pleased him to imagine that the couple who were now so enraptured with each other would someday come to their senses and split. Maybe one of them would get tired of the other and end the romance and all that went with it. It was a spiteful thought, but it pleased him nonetheless.

Chalmer took a deep breath. Making an effort to act casual, he made his way to Trowler's booth and, without an invitation from Trowler to join him, sat down across from him. With his words fumbling around on his tongue, his voice caught, but after a few seconds he regained his composure. "I hear you're the fella that was makin' it with my wife when she was still married to me," he said in a loud voice, making sure the patrons in the cafe and the heavy-set waitress who was making her way to the booth could hear him. Chalmer waved her off.

Caught completely off guard, Trowler mumbled and sputtered in an attempt to swallow a gulp of hot coffee that burned on his tongue. He quickly let the coffee mug drop to the table, clearly not knowing how to quell the accusation of this man across from him. His eyes darted about to reassure himself that others in the cafe weren't staring at them. After all, he was an important elected official and couldn't afford to have any voters think anything but the best about him.

Chalmer lowered his voice, goading the two-timing rascal. "Does your wife know anything about that? Does she, huh?" His words came out in a rapid-fire staccato clip. "I understand she holds the purse strings--got family money. Is that how you could afford a campaign to get yourself elected? What if she somehow found out about your little tryst or maybe trysts, or maybe you just call them dalliances." He was proud of himself for coming up with this big word. "After all, who knows, maybe there are others even more enticing," he continued unrelentingly. "You couldn't exactly say my ex is a prize catch, now could ya? Just interested in a little extra-marital sex, huh, and with how many? You must have quite an uncontrollable sex drive. Is that it, huh? On the last two sentences, he raised his voice enough for all the restaurant's customers to hear.

Trowler's face turned pale and he stuttered, his voice dropping to a whisper. "Are you threatening to tell my wife?"

"Well, now, I didn't exactly say that, did I?"

Trowler glared at Chalmer's badge, his expression contemptuous, his voice surly, and his gestures belligerent. "Let me tell you something, Mr. Important *Sheriff*, if you say anything, you'll be history. Understand? I've got connections," he hissed between his teeth. His cold blue eyes squinted as if he might be ready to kill. His hands knotted into fists.

"That sounds like a threat to me. Better watch it." Chalmer would have liked to smash Trowler's handsome face in and give him a punch in that flat gut of his. Instead he swallowed hard, released a sarcastic snort, and huffed, "You know what? You're a real horse's ass. No, on second thought, the comparison is an insult to the horse's anatomy." He got up and left.

By the time he got back in his car, he was shaking. He wished he'd never seen Trowler. That old inadequate feeling engulfed him. But then again, it never left him. It was always there just under the surface, ready to rear its ugly head. In the looks department, he was no match for Trowler. And he sure didn't have that slick, arrogant air about him. He decided that Trowler was the kind who could make black look white, and he hated the bastard. What chance did he have when Trowler decided to turn his charm on Sally? Not any, and he knew it. He grappled with that awful, hopeless dilemma. He wished he'd left well enough alone and stayed away from here. But then again, maybe he'd made the bastard worry a little, just thinking that his philandering ways might be catching up with him and his moneyed wife would find out. He had only guessed that Trowler's wife was the one with money, but he knew that he'd hit the nail on the head as soon as he'd seen the look on Trowler's face when he mentioned it.

Chalmer drove back to Rothersby in a glum mood. Why couldn't he just accept the inevitable and leave it alone? But somehow he knew he couldn't. Even if Trowler got tired of Sally and she came crawling back to him, he knew in his heart he'd take her back. That made him all the more disheartened. He wanted to hate her, but he didn't. He still loved her. He didn't want to, but he did, and that hurt like hell. It was enough to make a grown man cry.

Chapter 24

JIMMY AND JENNY NORTON

Fitful dreams disturbed Chalmer's sleep that night. They were a jumble of recurring images and voices--one after another--of Sally, Trowler, that cute couple at the cafe, Struthersville, Pewzer's dead body, and Hobbs telling him of Sally's unfaithfulness. His problems were pulling him apart with his loyalties split between his job and his personal problems.

When he awoke, he knew he had to get back to Struthersville. Work was good for the soul, and he needed something good at that moment--anything but bad dreams and dwelling on Sally.

As usual, the ubiquitous whittler sat on his bench, whittling away, but making nothing, going nowhere, accomplishing nothing. That's how Chalmer's felt when he and McIntire approached him. Chalmer knew he was no closer to solving Pewzer's murder than the day he had first examined his dead body. He just seemed to be whittling away with nothing but scraps falling to the ground, accomplishing no more than the whittler. There were just too many possible suspects. And now here he was again trying to drum up even more possibilities. Like his failed marriage, why couldn't he just leave it alone and forget about it? Nobody would care. But the trouble was, *he* would care. His sheriff's position was the only bit of self-respect he had left, and it was his job--what he had been elected to do. He realized, however, that he wouldn't be very popular if he arrested someone for the murder. Too many people were relieved and quite happy that Pewzer was dead and buried six feet under. Well, maybe not six feet, but close enough.

"Have ya thought of any more people that had a grudge against Pewzer?" Chalmer asked the whittler.

"Yeah, I've been thinkin' on that."

"And what have ya come up with?"

"Well," the whittler drawled, creating an aura of suspense as he forced Chalmer to wait for the information.

In the meantime, McIntire grew impatient and stood on one foot and then the other. Mocking the whittler, he said in an exaggerated drawn-out drawl, "Well, what? What's takin' ya so long to spit it out?"

That comment didn't sit well with Chalmer. He scowled at McIntire. "Shut up, you imbecile, and give him time. He's been a lot of help." As if scolding a small child, he said, "If ya don't know how to behave, I'll leave ya back at the office from now on."

McIntire had been properly put in his place, and for the first time, Chalmer observed a hint of a lazy, lopsided grin on the whittler's normally expressionless face.

"Well," the whittler said, "I know of another person who threatened to kill him. Don't know if he meant it or not."

"Who was that?"

"Ray Norton."

"And what did Pewzer do to him?" At this point, Chalmer wouldn't be surprised by anything.

"It had to do with his twins."

"His twins?"

"Yeah, they're not too smart, well, neither is Ray, and when Pewzer needed someone to help him on the farm after the split--you know--after Opal and the kids left, he hired Jimmy and Jenny. That's the twins' names. They probably needed the money 'cause about all they got to live on is a government check, and Ray claimed the farewell lady--that's what he called her--was threatenin' to cut 'em off if Ray didn't get hisself a job. Them there twins stayed with Pewzer out on the farm for a few days. He was doin' farm work, and she was takin' care of the chores in the house. Well, one day Jimmy came in the house unexpected like and caught Pewzer tryin' to put the make on Jenny, if ya know what I mean. Well, he cussed out Pewzer and grabbed Jenny by the arm, and they was out of there. They walked all the way back to their own farm. That's about five miles on the opposite side of town. Well, when they told Ray, he saddled up his horse and paid a little visit to Pewzer. You know, he's as mean as a bitin' dog when it comes to protected them kids of his, especially after their mother died. I hear tell he gave Pewzer a good thumpin' and threatened to kill him if he ever touched his girl again."

That little narration roused McIntire's interest. "Did he ever bother her again?"

"Can't say, but if he ever tried to, I bet he'd have been dead meat."

Chalmer had just been given another reason for somebody to hate Pewzer and another reason to let sleeping dogs lie, but he asked, "Can ya give me directions to Ray Norton's farm? Maybe I'd better go have a chat with him."

"Whatcha want?" Jenny asked when she answered the door. In her arms she was holding a gray tiger-striped cat that purred loudly as she stroked its back. The screen door to the dilapidated, unpainted house was hanging by one hinge. Her crooked teeth, dirty brown hair, and a dress that barely stretched over her emaciated body struck Chalmer as the result of poverty with no way out. The dress, unquestionably made from printed feed sacks, had probably been a hand-me-down from someone who pitied the poor girl. It looked as though the dress could have used another feed sack. Perhaps unaware of just how bad she looked, she seemed to be impressed by McIntire's tall height. She looked his rangy body up and down as if she couldn't get enough of him.

Chalmer said, "I need to talk to your dad, if he's available." Still looking at McIntire, she told him that her dad and brother were down by the barn putting up hay.

Fearing they would be attacked by a large, viciously barking dog, they cautiously walked toward the barn. As it turned out the mutt's bark was worse than his bite, and it sidled up to McIntire, who talked to him and gave him a pat on the head.

Chalmer and McIntire found Ray Norton and his son soaked with perspiration. They were tossing hay into the steaming-hot barn with pitchforks. "I'm Sheriff Chalmer, and I need to ask ya a couple of questions, if ya don't mind." He didn't know what he'd say if Norton said he did mind. He'd never before thought of the chance of that happening.

However, Norton put his pitchfork down, hooked one thumb in his overall pocket, and said, "Ask away. Me and my boy need the rest anyhow." Except for his height, Jimmy seemed to be a carbon copy of his dad, with hair that needed cutting, a sunburned face, a bulbous nose, and small ears pinched close to his head.

"I hear ya once threatened to kill Ekbert Pewzer. Can ya tell me about that?"

"Shore can. He was tryin' to put the make on my Jenny, but thanks to Jimmy here, he didn't get very far. I would've killed him if he'd ever laid a hand on one of my kids again, and I went over there and told him just that." He wiped his sweaty brow with the back of his hand. "But if you're a thinkin' I killed him, you're wrong. I didn't! But I'm glad he's dead!"

"Did ya have any more trouble with him after that?"

"Shore didn't. I reckon I scared him pretty good--beat him up pretty good too, and proud of it." He spewed out the words as if he didn't care what the sheriff thought.

Chalmer rubbed sweat off his forehead with a smelly handkerchief he had pulled out of his hip pocket. He felt he was pretty good at watching people, judging their reaction, and figuring out if they were lying. He decided that Ray Norton, who appeared to be as tough as the burr on an old oak tree, was probably telling the truth. "Thanks for talkin' to me. I'll let ya get back to your hay." He and McIntire were relieved to be out of the hot barn.

Chapter 25

DOC SIMPSON

Arriving back in Struthersville just as Doc Simpson was parking his car close to his office, Chalmer pulled up beside him, got out, and stuck out his hand to introduce himself. "You're a hard man to catch. Where ya been?"

"Oh, just about everywhere. You know how babies keep being born and I'm the one to call--still a few home deliveries, even after all these years." Chalmer wondered just how many babies the doc had delivered in all his years of practicing medicine. "But today I just got back from Rothersby--had to take a kid to the hospital. His appendix was about to bust. I got him there in time, and he's going to be all right."

Chalmer could sense the note of self-importance and satisfaction in Doc's voice. He was still saving lives and took special pride in that. Chalmer could also smell the hospital ether that still clung to Doc Simpson's wrinkled pants and long sleeved shirt. A long sleeved shirt of all things in this hot weather!

Chalmer admired the doctor for being dedicated enough to this small town that he still made house calls. He knew the doc's practice couldn't be very lucrative--that he was in it for the good he could do for the people who lived in Struthersville or on farms that weren't too far out. But he wondered how up to date the doc was and how much longer he'd be able to maintain a practice. He teetered around with stooped shoulders and shaky hands as he went inside his office with the door standing wide open, like it had been the other times Chalmer had been in town. The two officers of the law followed him inside.

"What can I do for you and this strapping big fellow you've got there by your side?"

"Oh, this is my deputy, James McIntire. I just needed to ask ya if ya ever had to patch up anybody that Ekbert Pewzer had done in and if he ever bothered you?"

"Nope, he never bothered me, but I've had to sew up a few that he did bother, but only one that I'd consider hurt real bad."

"Who's that?"

"His name's Johnny Lockwood. One day he came in here with blood streaming down his face and with a big gash in his arm. He was bawling like a baby and said this Pewzer fella had chased him right down the middle of Main Street, calling him a big sissy and that sissies didn't belong in Struthersville. Anyhow, he'd caught up with him and tripped him with his face falling flat into the gravel. Then he gave him a pretty mean kicking while he was down. Now, Johnny's a bit different. He, uh, he likes men, if you know what I mean. That's kind of asking for trouble in this town."

That's when McIntire got curious. "What's wrong with that? I got men friends. That don't mean I'm askin' for trouble."

Chalmer gave McIntire a sharp stare, shook his head, and said to the doc, "You'll have to overlook him. He's still wet behind the ears."

"Uh? What're ya talkin' about?" McIntire sputtered.

With a disgusted look, Chalmer said, "Doc means he'd rather have a boyfriend than a girlfriend or a wife."

"Shucks, what kind of a man is that?"

"Exactly! Now you're catchin' on. Now, why don't ya keep your yap shut and let the doc finish his story." Chalmer couldn't believe that McIntire had lived this long and didn't know what a queer was.

"The whole time I was stitching Johnny's head and arm up, with an awful lot of stitches, I might add, he was in terrible pain, just a screaming that he'd kill Pewzer if he ever got the chance."

"Do ya think he could have done it?"

"No way. I'd be surprised if he's strong enough to kill a rat."

"But do ya think he could have paid somebody to do it?"

"Sure don't. He's not got any money. Why, he's still not paid me. He offered to bring me a chicken or some vegetables from his garden to pay me, but I told him to forget it. I get lots of things like that instead of money. Now if he'd offered to bring me some wood or cut my lawn for me, that would've been a different story."

"What about any of the others that you had to patch up a little. Could they have done Pewzer in?"

"I don't think so. None of the other cases were very serious."

"Well, thanks for answerin' my questions. I'm just tryin' to dig up all the facts I can, and you've been a big help." Chalmer started to leave, thought for a few seconds, and then reluctantly said, "By the way, Doc, don't ya think it's kinda risky, or even dangerous, for that matter, for ya to leave your office unlocked when you're out on one of your calls?"

"Ah, a lot of people want to come in here and weigh on my scales, so I leave it open for things like that. There's not anything in here that anybody'd want."

"What about the medicine?"

"It's all locked up in that cabinet over there in the back room."

Chalmer peered through the door and looked at the glass doors to a metal cabinet with a padlock on it. Good-sized jars with pills inside were locked away inside the cabinet. A few syringes and some liquid medicine of some kind were also inside. He couldn't help wondering if Doc Simpson any longer knew what any of it was for.

"Well, you know your business better than I do." Chalmer patted his belly. "I think I'll take advantage of your scales while I'm here and weigh myself." He stepped on the scales and was pleased to see that he'd lost a few pounds, but why wouldn't he with the divorce and him just grabbing something to eat on the run? This murder investigation was keeping him plenty busy. He wondered how the doc could keep up with everything as old he was. "Doc, thanks for the information, and don't get too busy takin' care of other people that ya forget to take care of yourself."

Driving back to Rothersby in deep concentration, Chalmer finally said, "I've got to take a few days break from this shit. As my dad used to say, I'm plumb tuckered out. The farther I dig into it, the farther I fall behind." He decided it'd be good for him to maybe go to a local baseball game and talk to people who weren't suspects. He needed to live like a normal person for a change. It seemed that he was always interviewing somebody, but for what? It just gave him more work to do, and he was tired. "We're not gettin' anywhere anyway."

He looked at McIntire. "You need to take a break too. Don't ya want to go on a date or somethin'--maybe go to a movie. I hear that new movie *Picnic* is pretty good."

"Yeah, I've been thinkin' about askin' Donna Wasmer out, but I can't quite get up the nerve. I'm afraid she'd turn me down."

Chalmer knew Donna, and liked her a lot. "Well, you'll never know till ya ask her."

"But if she says yes, what do we talk about? That worries me. I never know what to say around girls."

"Well, it seems to me you should have plenty to talk about with what we've been doin'. But it's been my experience that you just need to be interested in a woman and ask her a lot of questions. She's sure to want to talk about what she's been doin' and what she thinks about stuff. Now why don't ya call her up and ask her out, and then don't bother to come in tomorrow." Chalmer knew he was the last person on earth that should be giving advice about women and relationships. He couldn't even hold his own marriage together.

"Maybe I'll just do that."

Chalmer decided to go by the Big Wig drive up and grab a Big Wig sandwich to take back to his apartment and have the one cold beer he usually allowed himself each day. He sure didn't need a bigger beer gut than he already had.

As he sat swigging his beer and eating the sandwich so fast that he barely tasted it, he couldn't get his mind off the investigation. Something was bothering him, and if he could figure out what it was, he could probably wrap this case up. But right now, he needed to get his mind off of it. Maybe a Little League baseball game would clear his head.

Chapter 26

A REPRIEVE

Glad to be away from the investigation and thoughts of the divorce, Chalmer stepped up on the stands at a championship Little League game. He'd always liked baseball, and he liked kids even more. That old longing for a son of his own came roaring back to him. Sally had left him, but at that moment he wished he'd left her years ago and met and married a woman who wanted children. But then again he loved Sally--still did. Nature played strange tricks on people. As much as he tried to insulate himself from the hurt, it was always with him, leaving him filled with remorse. What had he done wrong? Not that she hadn't told him often enough. Apparently he'd done everything wrong--even enough to drive her to another man.

He was greeted by a few friends and lots of acquaintances, slapping him on the back and asking him a myriad of questions. The questions just kept coming:

"How are you, old buddy?"

"Haven't seen you for a while."

"Are ya doin' all right since the divorce?"

"How long's it been?"

"Have ya latched on to another woman yet?"

He didn't bother to respond to the inquiries about his divorce. It was easier to pretend he didn't hear the questions or to answer with a grunt, a nod of the head, or a simple "okay."

Many people were curious about the murder investigation:

"You found out who done it yet?"

"Do ya reckon you'll ever pin it on somebody?"

"Do you have any good leads?"

Calmer gave a brief answer to those questions. "Nope. It's goin' at a snail's pace," and then he clammed up. But he thought dismally that it was going slower than a snail's pace, because it was going nowhere at all. At least snails made a little progress. He made absolutely none.

Even the Democrat he'd defeated for sheriff said, "I don't envy you, old man, having to track down a killer. I bet you never imagined you'd be doin' that."

"Nope, sure didn't."

"Well, I'm glad you're the one dealin' with it instead of me." For the first time Chalmer wished he'd lost the election. Life would have been a lot simpler, but then what would he have done with his time? He hated working at that boat factory day in and day out.

As soon as the players had finished warming up and the game got underway, everyone became so engrossed in the game that they quickly forgot about Chalmer. He could settle back and enjoy the action, but he was soon lost in reverie.

He reflected on how grouchy he had been lately with McIntire. He was frustrated and on edge by his lack of progress, but he had no right to take it out on his young deputy. When he thought about the word *grouchy*, it reminded him of the time McIntire was twelve years old and had sprayed MEAN in red paint on a neighbor's garage door. The neighbor had caught him in the act and called the police.

Living only a few houses down in the same nice neighborhood of small post-World War II houses, Chalmer had always liked the friendly, lonely-acting boy. It seemed his parents were too involved with their own activities to care much about what he did. They simply ignored him as long as he stayed out of their way.

Chalmer had taken it on himself to assure the neighbors and the police that he'd keep an eye on the boy--take him under his wing, so to speak. He even helped McIntire repaint the garage door that he had vandalized.

No juvenile charges were filed, but when Chalmer asked McIntire why he had done such an awful thing, he was told that the neighbors were always yelling at him about something--that he couldn't even play with a ball without them griping that the ball might break out a window. He said he started to write *grouchy*, but wasn't sure how to spell it, so he wrote MEAN.

Chalmer smiled a little just thinking about that. McIntire hadn't been the smartest kid on the block, but he was likable and tried his best to please. Regretting that he'd never had a son of his own, Chalmer started calling him My Little Buddy McIntire and took him to a few movies and plenty of local ballgames, like the one Chalmer was now attending. He had real affection for the boy and would somehow be lost without him.

Years later when Chalmer was elected sheriff and McIntire turned eighteen, Chalmer swore him in as a deputy. He thought again that he may not be old enough to be a deputy, but in this county it didn't matter. Nobody else would have wanted the job anyway.

The roar of the crowd responding to a homerun by the home team brought Chalmer's focus back to the game, but he vowed to be more patient with his former Little Buddy McIntire.

After a winning effort by the local team, Chalmer was invited by a couple of old friends to join them for a beer at Susie's Bar and Grill. He drank too much, but it felt good to laugh and forget about his troubles.

Chapter 27

A SECOND DAY OF REST

On his second day away from the investigation, Chalmer stretched out to enjoy a murder mystery on his television set, which seemed more blurred than usual. He was almost asleep, still recovering from a hangover headache, when the doorbell rang. Half dazed, he wondered who that could be. Nobody ever came here. He hoped it wasn't that McIntire wanting to tell him about his date. Chalmer needed a break from him almost as much as he needed a break from Pewzer's murder. This investigation was gnawing on him.

Groggily, he stumbled to the door, where he found Sally standing there with a scowl and a spiteful look in her eyes. Her dishwater blond hair was neatly in place, but too much makeup failed to cover the dark circles beneath her blue eyes.

Chalmer said nothing. What was there to say? He wanted to ask her what she was doing here, but thought that might sound overly rude. He stood rooted to the floor, frozen in the moment, inhaling a faint drift of her familiar perfume. While she struggled for words, the silence between them became increasingly ominous.

"Well, aren't you going to ask me to come in?" she finally demanded.

"Oh. Oh, sure. Come in." He watched her as she scrutinized the apartment. It was strewn with dirty clothes. The floor hadn't been swept in days, probably weeks. Dust covered what little furniture he had in his furnished rental apartment. He knew Sally was a neat freak. He could just hear her squawking about the filth and how much of a slob he was. He'd heard it all before. He was embarrassed, but so be it. She didn't live with him anymore, and it wasn't any skin off her back. From the sofa, he removed a dirty shirt that still reeked from the odor of spilled beer and stale cigarette smoke.

"Have a seat," he mumbled. She didn't sit down. "To what do I owe this honor?" he asked flatly, his jaw hardening and his eyes turning cold, "and what happened to lover boy?"

Her face flushed, her temper flared, her eyes filled with fury, and she flashed him a look that would make a mean dog turn tail and run. "To be right honest," she hissed between gritted teeth, "I want to know what you said to him. You sabotaged our relationship, didn't you! I know you did!" Her tirade went on and on. "It couldn't be anyone else, so you might as well admit it! And I hate you for it!"

Chalmer became just as angry, his body stiffening. He wanted to hurt her like she'd hurt him. "I guess ya know he's married, as if you'd care! You surely don't think you're the only one he's havin' an affair with! He's probably congratulatin' himself for his many conquests, and you're just stupid enough to fall for his slick lines. Why do you think you're so special that you'd be the only one he'd have anything to do with!" The longer he talked, the louder his irate voice became.

"Oh, how could you! For your information, maybe I'm more desirable than you give me credit for. That's the trouble with you! You think the world revolves around you. Well, I've got news for you, it doesn't! You're a big nobody, and even with that hot-shot badge and uniform of yours, you're still a nobody! And just look at this place! It's a pigsty--a filthy pigsty, and you're a no-good slob." Her hands flung to her hips. "And why don't you get a telephone! Why should I have to come all the way over here just to give you a piece of my mind!" With that, she stomped the few feet to the door, flipped her hair back, flung her head to one side, and yelled back over her shoulder, "And from now on, keep your damn nose out of my business! What I do is no concern of yours!" She slammed the door shut so hard that the butt-filled ashtray rattled on the coffee table.

Chalmer cringed. He had never heard her swear before. He was more bitter and more distraught than ever. What right did she have coming here with her acid accusations and calling him a slob and a nobody, like she owned the place and was something special? He'd never lived up to her expectations, and she had constantly made it clear that he wasn't smart enough to suit her. Well, he was working on that. In the back of his notebook, he kept a list of big words that he heard or read in the newspaper. Maybe he didn't spell some of them right, but he usually got close enough to pronounce them whenever he had a chance to use one of them. He didn't much like for people, especially Sally, to think he was stupid.

Not long after Sally's hasty exit, the doorbell rang again. Expelling a deep huff of breath, Chalmer got up, steadied himself, and went to the door. "What does she want now?" he growled to himself. However, when he opened the door, there stood McIntire. "Can I come in? I need to talk to ya."

Chalmer didn't want him to come in. In fact, he didn't want anybody to come in. He just wanted peace and quiet, but what could he say? He rubbed his aching head. "Sure. How'd your date go?"

"That's what I want to talk to ya about." McIntire scratched his head and squinted. "Not so good, I guess. She wouldn't let me kiss her."

"Well, that's not too unusual on a first date." Chalmer shook his head and grimaced, thinking how trivial McIntire's problem was compared to what he was dealing with. He didn't say it aloud, but he felt sure McIntire would be better off if he never got involved with a female. They were trouble from the word go, as he well knew, especially after just dealing with his irate ex. He wanted to dismiss the whole thing, but he continued to listen to McIntire, whom he had mentored for most of his young life.

"But that's not all. She said her dad wouldn't let her go out with me again."

"Umm, why not?"

"He said he didn't like the idea of her ridin' around in that old rattle-trap of a car of mine. He said I wasn't good enough and wouldn't ever amount to nothing, and . . . and I guess he's right."

"Umm, that's too bad. But, listen, boy, don't even think like that. My ex told me often enough that I'd never amount to anything, and just look at me. I was elected sheriff of this whole county. Look at it this way, my boy, there'll be others. As they say, there's lots of fish in the sea, and there's lots of gals that'd like to go out with a good-lookin' guy like you." Chalmer's thoughts focused on Sally. He needed to take his own advice. Would he ever find somebody else? Would he ever *want* anybody else? How could you hate someone one minute and love her the next? Relationships made no sense--no sense at all.

"Do ya really think so? I shore hope you're right." Feeling better, McIntire said, "Well, I'll be moseyin' along." He headed toward the door, then turned back. "You don't look so good. Are ya sick?"

"Naw, I'm okay. I just need to rest up a bit."

Chalmer called that afternoon to have a telephone installed and requested that the number be listed. He figured a telephone might spare him from these unwanted visitors and having to deal with them face to face.

Chapter 28

THE JUVENILE

The next morning, Jenkins squeezed his trim body into the office just in time to answer the phone. "I'll be right there," he said urgently and let the receiver drop. "There's a fight over by the park--the one just two blocks from here. I'll handle it," he said as he rushed back out the door.

When his car pulled up to the curb, a scrawny-looking kid was just getting off a bigger boy on the ground. Blood seemed to be everywhere. A woman was screaming at Jenkins to arrest the kid. "Look what he did to my boy!" she shouted as she attempted to help her son up.

"I'll take care of it," Jenkins assured her. "Do you need some help with him?" he asked, nodding toward the boy who was struggling to get to his feet.

The woman shook her head. "No, but I insist you arrest him! Look what he did!" she shrieked, pointing to her son's torn shirt and bloody nose.

"I'll take care of it, ma'am," Jenkins said again in an attempt to pacify her. He took hold of the scrawny boy's arm and guided him to the car.

On the way to the sheriff's office the boy never lifted his eyes, sitting silent and sullen. Jenkins, with his teeth clamped tightly together, didn't utter a word--no reprimand, nothing. It wasn't his place. Chalmer could handle this.

Once inside the office, Jenkins half shoved the kid into the empty chair. "He's all yours, sheriff. He beat up another kid, and did a pretty good job of it. The kid's mother insisted that I arrest him."

"What's your name?" Chalmer asked the boy, whom he figured to be about fourteen years old.

"Lloyd."

"Lloyd what? Ya do have a last name, don't ya?"

"Lloyd Brown."

Chalmer slowly took a drag off his cigarette and blew the smoke in the air. The boy immediately started coughing. Without raising his eyes, the boy muttered, "Sorry. Asthma."

"Oh," Chalmer said, and snuffed out a cigarette that had only one puff drawn from it. "How old are ya?"

"Sixteen."

Chalmer was surprised. The boy looked as if he might be malnourished. "Now, why don't ya tell me what happened."

"Ain't much to tell."

"Well, I'd like to hear it anyway."

With his head down in a refusal to meet Chalmer's eyes, the boy began reluctantly to tell his side of the story.

"That boy's always pickin' on me and callin' me names when I go outside. I try to look real careful like before I go outside to see if he's around anywheres close."

After a drawn-out pause with Chalmer waiting patiently, the boy wiped dried blood from his nose with his dirty hand. Jenkins handed him a tissue, and after another brief delay, he continued. "Anyhow, I guess this time I messed up. I didn't see him and was just walkin' down the sidewalk close to my house, and there he was. He shoved me off the sidewalk and said I wasn't allowed to walk there--that it was his sidewalk. I got back on the sidewalk and started to walk away. That's when he jumped in front of me and punched me hard--real hard--in the nose. Ya can see the blood." A look of grim determination took over his beleaguered face. "Anyhow, I got enough of it and I lit into him. I didn't care if he killed me. I just couldn't take no more." Through all of his narration, Lloyd sat expressionless.

"And then what happened?" the sheriff prompted.

"After a pretty good scuffle, I got him down and beat the crap out of him, that's what I done, and I'm proud of it." His voice became more confident and more defiant, but his eyes never looked up. "Ya can arrest me if'n ya want to, but he got what he deserved, and maybe I won't have to put up with him no more."

Chalmer looked at Jenkins. "How big was the other kid?"

"Lots bigger than this one, that's for sure."

"Then take Lloyd back to his house," Chalmer said, but felt obligated to admonish the boy. "But as for you, young man, stay out of trouble. All right?"

A slight grin made its way on Lloyd's lips as he got out of the chair. "All right, but I sure walloped him good."

As Jenkins and Lloyd went out the door, Jenkins asked, "Who's going to clean the blood out of my car seat."

Chalmer pointed to Lloyd. "He is."

After the door closed, Chalmer reflected solemnly about the days during his freshman year in high school, and in his mind he was fifteen again. That was a brutal year. He wasn't very big and a bit pudgy even back then, and there was this one bully who always picked on him. He'd never forget his name--Max Reemer. One time Max even yanked his pants down in front of some girls and yelled, "See how dinky it is," and laughed hysterically. The girls, one of whom Chalmer had a crush on, had turned away. Just recalling the humiliation made him blush to this day and thumped at his heart, hurting him way down deep in his soul. It had been a miserable year with the way he was made fun of and the many times his head had been banged against a door frame or his body shoved against a locker.

He had needed someone to confide in--someone to comfort him; however, he wouldn't have dared tell his foster father, a big tough guy who could have probably wrestled down a mountain lion. He would have just said he had more important things to worry about, called him a wimp, and told him to take care of his own problems. He could just hear him saying, "When are you going to buck up and be a man?" He always made it clear that he didn't like sissies--especially not in his household. His foster mother had cowered at his every tyrannical outburst--quaking at his every order. She wouldn't have been any help either. Besides, she had the responsibility of taking care of all the other foster children that paraded in and out of their home. Chalmer had often wondered how much money those foster children brought in. He always felt he was kept around because he was gritty enough, though barely big enough, to do all the outside work. It was a dismal place, but when the social worker came periodically to check on the children's welfare, it suddenly became a hunky-dory abode where everything was wonderful and everybody was happy.

Thinking about Lloyd and his bravado at taking on the bully, Chalmer let a half grin curl on his lips. He wondered why he hadn't had the guts to do what Lloyd had done. He admired the kid for being so tough--for tearing into the bully when he risked getting the crap beaten out of him.

Then Chalmer recalled with satisfaction his sophomore year. That was the year he had taken a growth spurt and muscled up somewhat from mowing yards the previous summer. He suddenly became bigger and stronger than Max the bully, who had gotten his growth early on. That ended the bullying and all the pain and torment that went with it. The best the bully could do was eye him with contempt but could never will his mocking words to come forth. Chalmer wondered if he would have beaten up Max Reemer if he'd tried anything physical, or even said anything. He couldn't quite imagine that scenario because he was a peaceful sort of guy back then and still was. He never liked confrontation and was the most unlikely person in the world to become an officer of the law.

The sheriff relit the cigarette that he had prematurely snuffed out in order to relieve Lloyd's anguish, took a long drag, and smiled out of one side of his mouth. Maybe there's justice after all. Now if he could just bring Pewzer's killer to justice that easily. Then it suddenly occurred to him that maybe, just maybe, he didn't have any pressing urge to bring anybody to justice. Maybe justice had already been served.

Chapter 29

CHASING LOOSE ENDS

The day was already shot to hell. He might as well drive back to Struthersville and see if he could tie up a few loose ends without McIntire tagging along.

He hadn't gone far when he noticed a dark, threatening cloud coming up in the west. He felt sure it would bring a rain--a badly needed one. The parched earth could use a good soaking, and even a little shower would settle some of the dust and cool things off a bit. An ominous feeling in the air engulfed Chalmer. However, the dark cloud wasn't any darker than the gloom in his heart.

It still looked like rain when he parked his car on Main Street in front of Phillips' store. A breeze was blowing, but it still wasn't raining. Maybe it would go around them. He looked across the street toward the barber shop. The whittler was nowhere in sight.

Burk came out of the grocery store chewing on a piece of baloney. Lyle wasn't with him. "How's it goin', old buddy?" Chalmer asked him, in an attempt to be friendly. "How ya been doin' in all this hot weather?"

Chalmer's friendliness seemed to rattle Burk. He stopped chewing, and his hands shook. "You're the sheriff, ain't ya? I ain't done nothin'."

"Well, I know that. Yeah, I'm the sheriff all right, but I just wanted to say hello to ya."

Burk seemed to relax a little. "Are ya findin' out anything?" he asked nervously.

"Not much. I hear Pewzer wasn't very nice to you and your brother. That's too bad. I guess you saw a lot of mean things out of him."

"Shore did. I even seen him grab the banker's wife and pinch her on the butt with him standin' right there."

"Oh, ya did? When was that?"

"Right before he got hisself killed."

Chalmer rubbed his chin. "Umm, that's interestin'. Calvin never told me anything about that happenin'."

"Well, it did 'cause I seen it. Ya know she always comes to town all dressed up and all."

"What did Calvin do?"

"Nothin'. What could he do?"

"You're right of course. What could he do?" Something clicked in Chalmer's mind. It was a lead pipe cinch that a banker would have enough money to pay for a killing. "I think I'll walk on down the street and go have another chat with Calvin."

Fear flashed in Burk's eyes. "Don't tell him I said nothin'."

"Ya can bet I won't. You take it easy now. By the way, how's that brother of yours?"

"Okay, only he don't hear much of nothin'."

"So I hear. Well, it's good talkin' to ya." Burk's shoulders relaxed, almost to the point of collapsing. Chalmer couldn't figure out how he and his sheriff's badge could have that kind of effect on anyone, but of course the insecure, down-and-out Burk wasn't just anyone.

Chalmer wanted to see the banker's reaction when he mentioned the little incident Burk had told him about. With all sorts of thoughts whirling in his mind, he waited for a customer to finish his business before he approached Banker Calvin.

When the customer left, Calvin acknowledged Chalmer's presence. "What can I do for you, sheriff?" he asked in his smooth, friendly banker's manner.

"Well, I've been checkin' around, as you well know, and somebody mentioned that Pewzer grabbed your wife and pinched her on the rear end with you standin' right there, and you didn't do a thing. I just wanted to hear your version of the story. Did ya have a little alteration . . . uh, altercation with him?" Chalmer quickly corrected himself, irritated that he got his big words mixed up with words that sounded similar.

Calvin's face turned red, and he rubbed his lips, as if reluctant to elaborate on the matter. Chalmer stood patiently, regarding him in skeptical silence, and looked him straight in the eyes. "Well, there's not much to tell. As a matter of fact, he did, and I didn't do anything, I'm ashamed to say." His voice trailed off. "But what could I do? Pewzer did whatever he wanted to do with impunity." Chalmer took note of the word *impunity*. That was a new one on him. He'd have to look it up and then record it in his little notebook. "And there wasn't anything anybody could do about it." Calvin continued. "Nobody dared to get into an altercation with that vile miscreant. He was invincible--or at least he thought he was. I guess he was wrong, wasn't he?'

"Were you mad enough to want a little retribution of your own?" Chalmer felt he should use big words that matched the banker's, but he wasn't sure he'd used the right word. Was it retribution or vindication? Well, no matter. That was beside the point.

Calvin seemed shocked at such a suggestion. "Absolutely not! Nobody would commit murder over a little thing like a pinch!"

Chalmer thought perhaps a pinch could be a little thing to some people but maybe not so little to somebody else, especially when it was demeaning enough to make a wife question her husband's propensity to protect her.

Just as Chalmer left the bank, lightning lit up the sky in long streaks that touched all the way to the ground. Booming thunder popped and cracked. He made a mad dash across the street, and just as he slipped inside the barber shop, a deluge of rain poured down and the electric lights flickered.

"Howdy, sheriff," the barber said. "Bad day to be out."

"Yeah," a customer in the chair added. "Not a fit day for anybody to be out and about. I figured we was gonna get a gully washer and it wouldn't be a fit day to get any crops in. A good day to get a haircut--'bout all it's good for."

The barber finished the haircut, brushed the customer's neck, took the cape off, and shook it out on the floor, with hair flying everywhere.

Chalmer was glad to be inside. "I see Snellings didn't make it today. That bench out there looks pretty lonesome without him."

The barber busied himself collecting his pay and sweeping up the floor. "Oh, he was here earlier, but when that big old cloud came up, he high-tailed it for home. He says he's scared to death of lightning--said one time it plumb knocked him off his feet."

"Does he live far from here?"

"Oh, a ways down the track--close to the old torn-down canning factory--lives in a little shack, but it's home to him. Anyhow, that's where he sleeps."

"Do ya mind if I sit here for awhile longer till the storm lets up?"

"Don't mind atall. Maybe you could bring us up to date on Pewzer's murder."

"I wish I could, but I'm gettin' nowhere fast. It seems like nobody, I mean nobody, liked Pewzer."

"That's for sure. Most anybody would've had reason to kill him if they got mad enough," the barber said.

"That's what I hear."

"Ya know, if ya got a real bad temper, it don't take much to set ya off, now does it, so why don't ya just let it alone and consider it good riddance?" the customer said, putting in his two cents' worth.

"I've wondered the same thing, but it's my job, and I'll be damned if I'm not gonna do all I can to find the killer. Or maybe it was killers, but I'd sure like to know who paid 'em off if that proves to be the case."

The lightning stopped as quickly as it had come, and the rain became no more than a light sprinkle. "Guess I'll be movin' along. Thanks for lettin' me set a spell."

"Any time. You're always welcome. We enjoyed talkin' to ya."

Chalmer looked across the street at the feed store. A young fellow was throwing a one-hundred-pound sack of feed, like it was no more than a ten-pound sack of flour, into the trunk of a car that was backed up to the loading dock. This was one place Chalmer hadn't been. He decided to have a chat with the owner. Maybe he'd learn something new.

He stepped up on the rain-splattered loading dock and introduced himself to an older man.

"I'm Clyde Jenkins, and this is my son Aaron. And everybody in town knows who you are. We don't miss much around here, especially when a murder's being investigated."

"Well, I'm workin' on it." He nodded in Aaron's direction. "Pleased to meet ya. I was just wonderin' if you all ever had any trouble with Pewzer."

"Nope. Never did." Clyde hesitated. "Well . . . maybe once. One time he ordered a sack of feed, and Aaron here loaded it in his pickup, and he just drove off without paying for it. Well, you can imagine that didn't set very well with us, so the next time he came in to get feed, I collared him real good and told him he wasn't about to get any more feed till he paid for the one he stole and from now on nothing would be loaded until we had cash in hand."

"And what did he say?"

"He sputtered around and got out his billfold. That's what he did. You know he wouldn't be any match for me or Aaron, let alone the both of us."

Chalmer looked Clyde and Aaron up and down. Both of them were the burly type--all muscle and brawn. "And ya never had any trouble with him after that?"

"Sure didn't," Clyde chuckled.

"I can see why. Well, thanks for talkin' to me. I think I'll mosey on down the street to the depot. It looks pretty quiet over there."

As he sauntered across the street and walked toward the depot, he heard a man shout, "Quit that, you little punk, or when I get down from here, I'll beat the livin' crap out of you."

Following the sound of the voice, Chalmer looked up to see a man up a telephone pole making some kind of adjustment. On the ground below stood a snarly boy taking aim with his BB gun and shooting at the man.

With a hasty approach, Chalmer walked up behind the obnoxious kid and grabbed him by the shoulders. "I'm the sheriff, and I could arrest ya for that."

The scalawag took off like he'd been shot out of a cannon.

"Are ya all right?" Chalmer yelled up at the repairman.

"Yeah, thanks a lot. He's a mean little bastard. Everybody around here calls him Freddie the Terror, and that's just what he is--a real terror if I ever saw one."

In the recesses of his mind, the sheriff speculated that this Freddie kid could someday turn into another version of Ekbert Pewzer. He hoped he wouldn't. "Well, maybe I scared him bad enough that he won't come back before ya get finished up there."

"Yeah, well, I think you took care of that."

"Then have a good day," Chalmer said before ambling toward the depot. The blazing sun had come out, and steam billowed up from the wet sidewalk, requiring deep ragged breaths. The sheriff sucked in his breath before entering the cluttered cubicle that the station agent called an office. At one time it must have served the town well. A board tacked to the wall displayed train schedules and tickets waiting to be sold.

The stooped agent laboriously rose from a paper-strewn desk when Chalmer came through the door. Poor eyesight prevented him from immediately spotting the sheriff's badge. "Do you need a ticket? Where are you headed?"

"No, I'm not needin' a ticket. I'm the sheriff, and I've not talked to you yet. Thought I'd chat awhile if you're not busy."

"Does it look like I'm busy? I've been here nigh unto forty years and believe me things have changed--changed a lot. I still get a few passengers going to Rothersby and other points west, but not many. Once in a while I sell a ticket to St. Louis. With all the cars on the road, passenger trains will soon be a thing of the past. Now the freight business is still good with the fish hatchery shipping out all those big metal containers filled with goldfish."

"Well, that's good." Chalmers wasn't much interested in the coming and going of the depot. "I'm investigatin' Ekbert Pewzer's murder."

"I heard about that. Of course, come to think of, everybody has."

"Did he ever come in here?"

"Nary a time."

At that moment, a young man came storming inside, all out of breath. He was sucking in great gulps of air. "Sheriff, they told me you'd come down this way!"

"Slow down. What's the matter?"

Me and another guy have been seein' to Carl Warlon, and he says he's just got to see ya--that he's got a confession to make. He says he's the one that killed that SOB Ekbert Pewzer. You'd better come quick!"

Rushing out the door and panting for breath, Chalmer could hardly keep up with the young man. "Where we goin'?" he wheezed.

"Over on the next street," he yelled back over his shoulder. "It's where Carl lives. It's a nice house. I reckon he's got money, but he's drinkin' it all up."

They crossed the railroad track and ran a block farther.

Even before Chalmer entered the door, he heard a blood-curdling scream. "Get them off me! They're gonna poison me! They're wrappin' around me."

Chalmer followed the young man and the sound of the screams into a small, wallpapered bedroom where a drunken, red-faced man lying in the bed appeared to be fighting for his life--fighting off demons that weren't there. Puzzled, the sheriff asked, "What's the matter with him?"

"He's havin' one of his fits, that's what. He gets drunk and thinks snakes are all over him."

Dumbfounded and not knowing what to say, Chalmer stared at the drunk, a man probably in his thirties. He'd never seen anything like it. "Ooh, that's bad. But where's the guy who's confessin' to murder?"

"Him."

"Him!"

The courier shook Warlon's shoulder. "The sheriff's here if ya got somethin' to say to him."

"You say you killed Ekbert Pewzer?" the sheriff asked.

Suddenly, the drunken man ceased his fighting. Apparently in his mind the snakes had crawled off somewhere else. His body was still shaking from tremors that wouldn't let go.

"Yeah, I killed him, sure as I'm here, and I can't live with the guilt anymore."

Chalmer was noticeably skeptical and felt considerably more than a trickle of irritation at being called to the scene. "Oh yeah? How'd ya do it?"

Wild-eyed and shaking and quivering like he was as cold as a snowball, he rasped, "I threw a snake on him. That's what I did. It was a real poisonous one too, and it bit him, but sheriff, I didn't mean to kill him. Honest, I didn't." What little color he had drained from his face.

"Now just calm down. What if I told ya he was beaten to death? There wasn't any snake that killed him, and you had nothin' to do with it."

"But . . . but I did. I know I did." He fiercely shook his head and flailed about.

"Maybe ya just imagined ya did, or maybe dreamed it. Yeah, maybe it was just your imagination playin' tricks on ya--like the snakes ya see when they're not really there. You know, ya should lay off that booze. It's not good for ya."

The man who had come to the depot to get Chalmer apologized. "I'm real sorry, sheriff. He sure convinced me that he had somethin' to do with Pewzer's murder. I guess he's farther gone than I thought. He didn't say he'd killed him with a snake, or I wouldn't have come after ya."

Chalmer looked at Warlon. He was a pathetic sight. How could a person get himself in that kind of shape? He hated that anybody had to suffer so, but that wasn't his problem. He couldn't change the plight of somebody that had brought so much misery upon himself and was helpless to change it. In his mind, it was a grave situation. What a thought, he suddenly realized. He hadn't intended for his thoughts to create a pun, but he knew this poor fellow was taking a shortcut to the grave.

The sheriff decided to get a bite to eat at the only eating establishment in Struthersville. It would save him from trying to cook up something when he got back to his apartment. He didn't cook much and when he did it tasted like glue, or maybe crap. Eating alone could be a depressing endeavor.

Inside the dismal place that wasn't the cleanest he'd ever seen, he was greeted by the proprietor and a few customers. Two teenagers with the sleeves of their tee-shirts rolled up as high as they would go played the pinball machine that rattled and pinged in the corner of the square room. One boy had a pack of cigarettes rolled into one sleeve. Everyone seemed eager to ask the sheriff questions. A murder didn't happen once in a blue moon in little places like this--maybe never--and Pewzer's demise would give the citizens something to talk about and speculate about for a long time--maybe years or even decades.

"How's it goin', sheriff? Any news to report?" a pudgy man with a head as slick as a bowling ball asked.

"Sorry, none whatsoever." Chalmer was tired of being assailed with questions, but he was even more weary of his inability to give anybody a positive report. It was at times like this that he felt like a failure, which was most of the time. He tried hard to beat back his inferior feelings at the lack of any progress.

He ordered a hamburger with extra onions, but he had a question of his own for the owner, who moved in sweeping motions, never wasting his muscles on two moves when one would do. "Did Pewzer ever give you any trouble, or did ya ever see him bother any of your customers . . . especially bad enough to make 'em want to kill him?"

Cleaning a table that had just been vacated, he shook his head. "Naw, can't say that he did, except the time he ordered a bowl of my chili. When he tasted it, he spit a big honker in it and claimed it wasn't spicy enough to suit him. He left here madder than and old wet hen. And he didn't pay for it either, and I was mad enough to kill him, if I could have."

"And what did you do?"

"What was there to do? A bowl of chili's not worth getting beat up for. And I sure had sense enough to know that Pewzer was capable of doing just that. I've got sense enough to know that I wasn't any match for him."

"He tweren't no good--no good atall," a little dried-up man, apparently bent from years of hard work, murmured under his breath. Chalmer wondered what misery Pewzer had wreaked on him, but he didn't ask.

The bald-headed man offered his opinion. "He sure was a mean son of a gun. Why, one time he spit in Aaron's coffee cup just for the heck of it."

Aaron, a gruff, lantern-jawed man sitting next to him gave him a hard jab with his elbow. His face turning red, he glared at Baldy and told him to shut up.

"Well, he did, and you know it," Baldy insisted. "And you took a big gulp of it before you knew what he did, and Pewzer left here just a hoohawin'. The dirty bastard!"

Chalmer contemplated what he would have done in that situation, but like the proprietor had said, "What was there to do?" He downed the hamburger. He loved onions, but onions made him think of Sally. She hated them as much as he loved them, and she had harped at him every time he ate them, especially when he accidentally expelled a big belch. He'd often said to himself that he'd rather give up Sally than to give up onions. He had even jokingly said the same thing to her. But now, he knew that wasn't true. He'd gladly give up onions to have Sally back the way they used to be. He'd give up anything, even his badge, to have things the way they once were when they were young and so much in love. It seemed like a life-time ago since they'd made love and whispered endearments to each other. A blend of desire and pain nearly overwhelmed him.

Chapter 30

THE CHEERLEADER

"Did ya find out anything new?" McIntire asked when Chalmer got back to the dinky office.

Chalmer was exhausted and frustrated. He didn't want to listen to any more questions.

"Nope. Not one little snippet."

"Not one little what?"

"Snippet. You know, not one little bit."

"Oh, I never heard that word before."

Chalmer started to chastise McIntire for being so dim-witted, but just then a young, attractive girl wearing a pink full-skirted dress with a crinoline petticoat meekly opened the door and asked if she could come in. She looked at McIntire and said she wanted to talk to the sheriff alone. Chalmer told McIntire, who was giving the girl the once over to the point of almost salivating, to get lost for a while.

"Have a seat," Chalmer said, gesturing toward the seat that McIntire had vacated. "What can I do for ya?"

He glanced around the office. Like his apartment, it was in dire need of a good cleaning. Dust covered almost everything, and the floors could use a good mopping. Under his breath he cursed the so-called county judges who were far too cheap to hire a janitor. He'd have to remember to tell McIntire to take care of the cleaning, but right now he was embarrassed that such a neatly groomed girl had to occupy this sorry excuse for an office--nothing more than a rat hole.

The teenager with jet black hair, dark eyes, and a clear ivory complexion clasped her hands together and fidgeted in the chair. She bit at the bright red lipstick that had been carefully smeared over her full lips. "Well." She paused. "Maybe I shouldn't be here."

"Well, now that you're here, let me be the judge of that. What is it that's got ya so nervous? They say I'm a good listener."

"I've come to ask a big favor of you--a really big favor."

"What's that?"

"I'm begging you to quit trying to find Ekbert Pewzer's murderer."

She had Chalmer's rapt attention. Why would a pretty girl like her care about his investigation? "Oh, why's that?"

She wiped the perspiration that formed on her forehead. "Because it has to do with a good friend of mine."

"What's this good friend's name? And for that matter, what's your name?"

"I can't say."

"Ya can't say, or ya won't say?"

"Both, I guess. I hope you understand." Chalmer noticed that she nervously twirled a class ring on her finger. He figured she was a recent high school graduate or maybe would be a senior the approaching year.

"Well, tell me, why does your friend care about my investigation?"

"Uh, you see it goes back to last winter. She was a Struthersville cheerleader and had just got off the bus after going to a basketball game and was walking home after dark about a mile away. She had missed her ride. That's when this Pewzer man came by and offered her a ride." She shuddered and stopped talking.

"Go on," the sheriff prompted softly.

"She got in his pickup." The girl sobbed, trying to squelch her surging emotions in order to continue. "She thought it'd be all right but he ripped at her clothes and . . . and he raped her. Then he dropped her off at her house."

"Why, that dirty . . . ." Chalmer didn't finish his sentence. He didn't talk that way around the fairer sex. "Try to pull yourself together. What happened then?"

"When she went in the house, her dad was waiting up for her and saw how torn her clothes were. She was crying, but she managed to tell him what had happened. He promised he'd kill the SOB. That's what he said. And then later she heard her dad talking to his brother, and they said they'd beat Pewzer to a bloody pulp if they ever got the chance."

Chalmer was on full alert. His interest had been piqued. "So why do ya want me to stop my investigation? And what's it to you?"

"Because she's my best friend and her mother died when she was young, and her dad's all she's got."

"You know, don't ya, that you've just given me a likely suspect. If ya hadn't said anything, I'd probably never known about these threats."

"That's just the problem. You would have, and I'm begging you to stop looking for the killer. Everybody's just glad he's dead anyway, and my friend, she doesn't know what she'd do if her dad ended up in prison."

"And how do ya think I would have known anything about this if ya hadn't told me?"

"Because she confided in a teacher, and I heard that as soon as school gets back in session, you planned to question some teachers. This one teacher'll be back in town as soon as her vacation's up. She's sure to tell you what she knows, and I'm begging--no, I'm pleading for you to just let it drop. Nobody'd care."

"Well, I'll think on that," he said to make the girl feel better, but he knew he couldn't let it drop, as much as Pewzer deserved what somebody had done to him. These men were the closest thing he had to a suspect. They'd threatened to beat him up, and that's just what somebody had done. He didn't know their names, but you could bet your bottom dollar that he'd find out.

The tearful girl got up to leave. "Please. I hope I've done the right thing," she sniffed before timidly skirting out the door.

McIntire soon came back into the office. "Wow, she was a pretty little thing. Now that's the kind of girl I like. What's her name?"

"She wouldn't tell me, and she wouldn't tell me the name of the girl she was talkin' about either. But I've got a notion--a real strong hunch--they're one and the same person."

"What do ya mean?"

"Well, she told me about how Pewzer had raped a friend of hers, but I'll bet a dollar to a doughnut that it wasn't any friend. I'd bet anything she was the one Pewzer raped. And I need to find out who she is and who her dad is--if I just knew how."

An appalling look registered on McIntire's face, but he managed to make a suggestion. "You could look in the Struthersville school annual."

Again, Chalmer felt inadequate for not thinking of that himself, but he didn't let on. "Oh, sure." he said. "Maybe the local library has a copy. They have things like that, don't they?"

A search of a collection of school yearbooks at the library, especially last year's, netted the picture Chalmer was looking for. There the girl was--a junior and a cheerleader. Her name was Denise Owensby. He had no doubt in his mind that this Denise had told what had happened to herself, not to a friend. It should be easy to track down her father. This was the closest thing he'd had to a substantial lead. As much as it might devastate Denise, he had to pursue it.

Chapter 31

THE CHEERLEADER'S FATHER

A few inquiries in Struthersville led the sheriff to Gilbert Owensby, who lived only a mile from town to the south. Chalmer learned that he was a supervisor at a boat factory in Rothersby, a different one from the one he had once worked at. Leonard, his brother, lived close by and worked on the line in the same factory.

Chalmer waited until nearly dusk before approaching Gilbert's house, a two-story structure, situated on a big, well-landscaped lot. He wanted to be sure Gilbert was off work so he could catch him at home. A big black and tan German shepherd and a tiny black dog barked but otherwise ignored him. An abundance of sweet-smelling purple petunias flourished in large pots on each side of the steps with honeybees buzzing nearby. When the rather tall, handsome Gilbert, clad in blue jeans, came to the door, Chalmer introduced himself and asked in a friendly, non-threatening tone, "May I come in? I'd like to ask ya some questions if ya don't mind."

Gilbert looked at the sheriff's badge. "Sure, come on in. What can I do for you?" He held the screen door open wide and motioned toward a chair. He took a seat across from the sheriff on the sofa.

Chalmer decided to just blurt out what he had on his mind. He wanted to see Gilbert's reaction. He'd always thought that actions or reactions spoke louder than words. "Did you have anything to do with Ekbert Pewzer's murder? Did ya beat him to death?"

At that moment Denise stepped into the room. Her jaw dropped, and a look of horrified shock and hatred and fear etched her face. Chalmer felt terrible. Law enforcement wasn't easy and was seldom kind. He mouthed the words, *I'm sorry*. She ran from the room crying.

With a somber expression, Gilbert looked down and rubbed his knees. "No, I didn't beat the bastard to death, but I wish I had." He suddenly bent over, and burying his face in his rough hands, he sobbed loudly. "The son of a bitch raped my little girl, and I'd have killed him sooner or later, but somebody beat me to it." He wiped his nose and eyes with the back of his hand.

"Can ya tell me what ya were doin' about the time he was killed?"

Gilbert looked up. "Yeah. That's easy. I was in Clamford, way up on the other side of Springfield. The company's opening up another plant up there, and me and my boss spent a whole week up there training new people."

"But ya could've come back down this way one of them nights, just long enough to kill Pewzer, couldn't ya?"

"Not very likely. Me and my boss shared a motel room while we were there."

"But maybe ya could've slipped out without him knowin' it. Maybe he's a sound sleeper, or maybe ya could've slipped somethin' in his drink."

"Well, why don't you just call him up and ask him."

"I just might do that." Chalmer rubbed his chin slow and easy like and then covered his mouth with his balled-up hand. "By the way, where was Denise stayin' while you were gone?"

"Over at my sister's. After what happened to her, I sure didn't want her staying by herself." Tears streamed down his face once again. It seemed to Chalmer that the incident had left him a broken man, and just thinking about it sent Gilbert spiraling into a heartbreaking frenzy. Chalmer immediately regretted causing the man so much anguish.

The sheriff had to admit to himself that he could have killed Pewzer if he'd had a daughter and Pewzer had raped her. "I reckon ya know I'll have to corroborate your story. Can ya give me the name of that boss of yours?"

"I'll do better than that. I'll give you his phone number and his address." Chalmer got out his little spiral notebook, his constant companion, to write down the information.

When Chalmer started for his car, Denise came from around the back of the house. As she approached him, fire was in her teary eyes and strands of her black hair stuck to her wet face. "How could you? You lied to me! You promised me you'd drop your god-awful investigation, and now you come here and accuse my dad!"

Chalmer found it difficult to say anything to this girl who was convinced that he had lied to her. The airless atmosphere that stood between them nearly suffocated him, but he managed to explain in a soft voice, "I didn't actually promise you anything. I said I'd think about it. That's all. I did think about it. And did you hear your dad's explanation? He wasn't even here at the time of the murder. You surely knew he was away on business. Why would you think otherwise?"

"I . . . I thought he just told me that so I wouldn't question what he was about to do."

"Maybe you should have more faith in your dad. Trust is important, ya know."

She gave him a searing look, did a sharp about face, and darted back behind the house.

Chalmer drove back to the office, where he called Hubert Snider, Gilbert's boss. Indeed, the week of Pewzer's murder, Gilbert and Hubert had been starting up a new factory. "Is there any possibility that Gilbert slipped out on ya one night?" Chalmer asked Hubert after identifying himself.

"Why? What's it any concern of yours?"

"Well, I'm investigatin' a murder that took place about the time he says he was with you. I thought he might be involved."

"Well, for your information, there's no way. I'm a light sleeper and I was awake most of the night tossing and turning in bed. Have you ever tried to sleep in a Holiday Inn bed? And besides, how could he have gone any place? I'm the one that drove. It was my car, and those keys never left me, not even for one minute. I can assure you of that."

Chalmer thanked him and hung up. Another dead end. He was back to square one. But he still needed to question the brother. Leonard may have done the deed for Gilbert while Gilbert had a slam-dunk alibi.

When he approached Leonard on the boat factory's assembly line and asked him how well he knew Ekbert Pewzer, Leonard immediately became defiant and hostile. "Do you think I had something to do with his murder? You think I did it, don't you! How dare you come here and accuse me of anything!" His tightened fists and his rapid-fire speech revealed just how angry he was.

"Now just take it easy, fella. I was just askin' ya a simple question. I didn't accuse ya of anything."

"Same as. I didn't have anything to do with any murder, and you don't have one shred of evidence that I did!"

His belligerence and raging temper took Chalmer aback. What a hot head! Why was he so upset over just a question? But Leonard was right of course. He didn't have one shred of evidence. And why would somebody commit murder for his brother, unless their bond was so close that Leonard would do anything for him, which could very well include murder? Maybe he had done it when he was sure Gilbert had an air-tight alibi.

Chapter 32

CONFESSIONS

As was the general rule, McIntire was waiting for Chalmer when he got back to the office. "I've got to talk to you. It's real important."

Chalmer's head felt like it was about to explode. His overloaded brain was bearing down on him, and now of all things, McIntire needed to talk to him. Tracking down a killer was getting to him. "What now?" he grumbled.

"She came on to me, really she did," McIntire stuttered.

"Slow down. Who came on to ya?"

"This girl. I can't even remember her name. I think it was Peggy. Anyhow, she was dressed up all sexy, short jean shorts and a low neckline--the works, and she didn't mind about my old car. She said she was just interested in the back seat, and before I knew it our clothes just went a flyin' and we were goin' at it hot and heavy and . . ."

"And ya did it, right?"

McIntire hung his head. "Yeah."

"For the first time, right?"

McIntire's face flushed.

"So what's the problem?"

"Well, golly durn, what if she's . . . you know . . . pregnant? I'm worried sick."

"Didn't you use anything?"

"It happened so fast I didn't have time to think."

"Well, let that be a good lesson for ya. Ya need to have enough sense to keep your pants zipped up."

"But what if . . . ?"

"Try not to worry about it," Chalmer said, trying to reassure him. "If she's that loose and heavy, she wouldn't know who the father was if she did get pregnant." He hoped he had alleviated some of McIntire's guilt, but he didn't think he could stand one more minute of his moaning and jabbering.

Just then the phone rang. At the other end of the line was a raspy-voiced female who identified herself as a nurse at the hospital. "Sheriff, there's a Mary Davis here. She wants to talk to you--says it's real important."

"You mean she's been hospitalized?"

"Her doctor admitted her just this morning. To be right honest about it, he doesn't expect her to last long. She's real sick--apparently has been for a long time."

"I'll be right over--just as soon as I can get there." Chalmer hung up, lifted himself out of his chair, and headed toward the door.

"Where ya goin?" McIntire asked. "Is it important? Can I go?"

"No, ya can't. You'd do more good stayin' just where ya are." Chalmer left without looking at McIntire or explaining where he was going. The hospital was no place for the young whippersnapper.

At the hospital Chalmer found Louella sobbing in the waiting room. When she saw him, she whispered, "It doesn't look good."

Mary was barely lucid when the sheriff walked into her hospital room. He could tell she was gasping for what would surely be one of the last breaths she'd ever take. He knew she was sick but hadn't realized just how close to death she was. "Mary, do ya feel like talkin'? The hospital called--said ya wanted to see me."

With much effort, she blinked her eyes open and wheezed, "I've got a confession to make. I can't go to my grave with this on my conscience."

Chalmer bent his head down closer to her to make sure he heard every word. "I'm listenin'."

"I paid . . ." she gasped. "I paid two men to kill Pewzer."

"I know this is hard for ya, but I need to ask ya some questions. Who did ya pay?"

With a nurse standing nearby, Mary closed her eyes. Chalmer thought she'd be unable to respond to his question, but he desperately needed answers.

Her eyes fluttered again. "Just two guys I stumbled on to." Her voice was no more than a barely audible whisper.

Chalmer pressed his eyebrows together. "How did ya stumble on to 'em?"

"They contacted me." Finding it difficult to go on, she paused for several seconds before continuing. "They'd heard I wanted somebody dead, and they needed the money."

"And where'd ya meet these guys to arrange for the murder."

"By Susie's Bar and Grill."

That made sense to Chalmer. The proprietor had seen a woman talking to a couple of men outside his establishment. "Who are they, and where are they now?"

She shook her head very slightly. "Long gone." She grasped for the hand of the nurse, who said, "Sheriff, you'd better go now. She's worn out, and you've already asked too many questions."

Chalmer held up his hand as if pleading for just one more question that was bothering him. He took Mary's other hand and asked, "Mary, I know this is painful for ya, but where'd ya get the money to pay the killers?"

"Divorce settlement," she gasped again after a lengthy pause.

Chalmer looked at the nurse and whispered, "Thanks for callin' me."

"Now maybe she can rest in peace," the attractive middle-aged nurse said as she stepped to the door with Chalmer. She walked into the hallway with him and smiled brightly.

He was immediately captivated by her smile and slim figure and made a special point to look at her left hand. She had no ring on her finger. She gave him someone to fantasize about. He longed to ask her out, but realized this wasn't the time or place. It would be completely inappropriate. Anyway, he was out of practice when it came to women, and he didn't have the nerve. Reluctantly, he said, "Thanks for calling me. Take good care of her."

He noticed that Louella was no longer in the waiting room and figured she'd gone to get some coffee or maybe a Coke. Surely she'd want to be with Mary when she breathed her last breath. He wondered where her mother and brother were. Maybe they hadn't had time to get there yet. It would be a sad day for all of them when she passed on.

Coming out of the air-conditioned hospital, he was hit by the hot, steamy air, and he was cursing himself for not asking the nurse if she'd like to have dinner with him sometime. But he was puzzled about something else. Did Mary confess to protect somebody else-- somebody like Louella or her mother, or perhaps Alvin? He'd do his best to unravel the mystery, but right now, all this was too mind-boggling to contemplate.

Chapter 33

AN UNEXPECTED VISITOR

Instead of going back to the office and facing McIntire's questions, Chalmer went straight to his dinky apartment where he swallowed two aspirins and stretched out on the ratty sofa with his arms covering his eyes. There was something about Mary Davis' confession that bothered him. Somehow, it didn't ring true. He wished it did. It would make his life a lot less complicated.

The sudden ring of his doorbell sent his head throbbing. Who could that be? Just what he needed! He desperately needed to be alone. He hoped it wasn't McIntire. "Who is it?" he yelled angrily while he was struggling to a sitting position.

"It's me." Chalmer recognized Sally's voice instantly--a voice that had been brutally directed at him often enough. "I need to talk to you." He wondered bitterly why she hadn't called. After all, she was the one who wanted him to have a phone put in.

He went to the door and cracked it open. Sally stood there with a covered dish in her hands. "I brought you a peace offering--lasagna," she said. "Your favorite."

"Oh." He was barely able to respond, with his words lodged somewhere in his throat. Yeah, sure, lasagna was his favorite all right, but how many times had Sally berated him for eating too much of it and nagged him about all the calories that made him way too fat?

"Aren't you going to take this? I made it especially for you?"

"And what's the occasion?" he asked caustically. "The last time I looked at a calendar, it wasn't anywhere near my birthday."

His words seemed to bounce off her before she recovered her equanimity and retaliated. "Well, you don't have to be so huffy about it. Can I come in? We need to talk."

Without responding, he opened the door wider, but didn't take the proffered lasagna. When she came in, she set the dish down on the coffee table after brushing an empty beer bottle and a scattered newspaper out of the way.

He sat down on one end of the sofa and motioned for her to sit on the other end. "And what is it we need to talk about? I thought you'd just about said it all the last time you were here."

"Uh, well, I guess I'm sorry about that." She seemed lost for words. "Well, I might as well get right to the point. I was just thinking it'd be a lot cheaper for both of us if you moved back in the house?"

"What! You want a slob like me to move back in with ya? I don't get it. What's the catch?"

"Well, you see, I'm kinda having a hard time making ends meet."

"Well, hotsy-totsy! And ya think I'm not! Ya mean ya can't make it on the alimony I'm payin'? Too bad. It's not easy for me either, ya know." He wondered why she didn't try to find a full-time job instead of that two-evening-a-week thing she was tinkering with. But then she'd never worked a day when they were married. She didn't have to, and she sure didn't have an impressive resume.

"That's the point. It's not easy for either one of us, but if we pooled our resources--uh, like roommates, of course--it'd be a lot easier on both of us. We could split the cost of the utilities and the like." Her lingering gaze warned him that something was amiss.

Chalmer looked at her with a quizzical expression. "Like roommates? Does that mean no sex?" It had been a long time--too long--since he'd had sex, and he was hurting without it.

"Yeah, that's what it means. You do understand, don't you?"

"It's as clear as mud." He opened his mouth to ask her if she couldn't find another lover boy--an unmarried one--to move in with, but thought better of it, and the thought died on his tongue.

"You know, it'd be advantageous for both of us. You wouldn't have to pay alimony, and I wouldn't have to keep our old house up for just one person." Looking vulnerable, she brushed her dark blond hair away from her forehead and waited for him to say something. When no response came, she said, "What do you think?"

"I think I need to think about it, that's what I think."

She got up to leave. "Well, that's fair enough, I guess. Let me know what you decide, and enjoy the lasagna."

He started to get up, but she said, "Don't bother. I'll let myself out. I do hope you know how hard it was for me to come here. I miss you."

Yeah, like a migraine, he thought. What was she up to now? As much as he still loved her, moving back in with her would be like moving in with a mountain lion. No, it would be worse. Mountain lions didn't nag; they just bit. He'd never have a minute's peace. Yeah, he'd think about it, but right now that would be as far as it would go. He went to the bathroom and gulped down two more aspirins.

That night, his recurring dreams about Denise Owensby accusing him of lying gave him little rest. That coupled with muddled up images of her father, of Mary Davis' confession, and of Pewzer's sparsely attended wake, and of Struthersville haunted him throughout the night. The dreams went on and on. Sally's lasagna hadn't set well with him either. It gave him heartburn, and he wondered if she'd deliberately put something toxic in it. With old inadequacies assailing him, he finally got up, threw the covers back, crawled out of bed, and flipped the television set on. Of course, in the wee hours of the morning, there was nothing on except static.

After taking some antacids, he dozed occasionally on the couch until it was time to get up.

Chapter 34

BACK AT THE OFFICE

On the short drive from his apartment to his office, Chalmer's contemplations soon returned to Mary Davis. It seemed unlikely that she just "stumbled" on to two men who needed money so badly that they were willing to kill for it. What would be the chances of that happening? Was she covering for somebody? Maybe her mother, or brother, or half- sister? If Mary was dying, she had nothing to lose. He couldn't very well imprison a dying woman, or a dead one. And that business about getting the money from a divorce settlement? Well, he'd have to check on that.

But right now, he needed to get the lowdown on what had been happening in the office. Probably nothing important, and he trusted Jenkins to cover for him, but still he was the sheriff, and he needed to know what was going on. Later in the week he had to testify in another domestic assault case, which had occurred two months earlier. He'd have to review that case to jog his memory a little. But it would probably be postponed again. He wondered why the court system moved so slowly, but he had a pretty good idea. The judges and the lawyers wouldn't want to miss out on a good game of golf at the country club.

When he entered his cubicle of an office, he glanced over the records and checked the meager jail population. He looked at Jenkins who was comfortably ensconced in the sheriff's chair behind the desk. Chalmer took the seat across from him. "Anything new been happenin' in my absence?" he asked.

"Same old, same old. Nothing we couldn't handle. Let's see now. Another domestic squabble, a couple of drunken disturbances, and the Squiggly boys are at it again. Oh, yeah, and a fight between two guys at that sleazy new beer joint on Adams Street, and wait till you hear this one--a cat that couldn't get down out of a tree."

"What!"

"You heard me right." Jenkins shook his head. "Now doesn't that beat all."

"What did you do? They surely didn't expect you to climb a tree and get a cat down, did they?"

Before Jenkins could explain how that scenario had been resolved, the door opened, and a man carrying a little boy walked in scowling. "Is she here yet?" he demanded to know.

"Oh," Jenkins said, "this is the day you're supposed to hand your son over to your wife, right?"

"Ex-wife," he corrected.

Chalmer looked up and shook his head. Why did his office have to supervise the visitation rights of divorced parents? Didn't they know what harm that would do to the kid? He had learned a lot about people since becoming sheriff, and he didn't much like what he'd learned. Why couldn't uncivilized people be civil for the sake of their kids, if for no other reason? Maybe it was better that he never had children, but he still wished he had.

The child's mother soon squeezed into the little office and without uttering a word, angrily snatched the child from his father and left. The father followed her out the door just as McIntire walked in.

He wanted to know what Chalmer had found out at the hospital. "Mary Davis confessed to Pewzer's murder, that's what," the sheriff dryly told him.

"Oh? How'd she do it?"

"Well, she said she paid two guys that she just stumbled on to."

"Then I reckon that wraps it up." Chalmer wasn't the only one who watched crime shows on television. McIntire did too, and that's what they all seemed to say at the end. It seemed appropriate.

"Not quite, my boy."

"What do ya mean?"

All the questions about Mary came whirling back in Chalmer's mind. Maybe verbalizing his doubts would clear his mind. "Why would she suddenly make a death bed confession? Would she have actually harbored that much hatred for Pewzer all this time and then suddenly needed to have him killed?" Chalmer thought awhile. "Of course, with some people hatred just festers and grows like a cancer. Maybe that was Mary's case. Pewzer robbed her of what was supposed to be the best years of her life, and now her young life is coming to an end." He scratched his head. "Was it a final act of revenge, or did she confess to protect somebody else? I wish I knew." Chalmer got up. "I think I'll take a walk. Maybe the hot air'll clear my brain."

Outside, he thought of the investigation from the beginning--all the way back to Susie's Bar and Grill and the bartender mentioning that he'd seen a light-haired woman talking to two men. That would give some credibility to Mary's confession. But two men wouldn't contact her out of the blue, would they? They couldn't just materialize out of nowhere. What men? And where did they come from? Chalmer's strides came to an abrupt halt. Bingo! Prison! He needed to know when Billy Davis was incarcerated and if he'd made friends who had killer instincts. But he didn't think Billy would have enough money to pay a killer since he was in prison for robbing a service station. A man with money didn't need to resort to robbery, and it was unlikely anybody would kill for free.

He wanted to know when Billy's family visited him and if they'd met any of Billy's fellow inmates. Surely they'd all had ample opportunity to meet up with some unsavory characters. Suddenly things began to fall into place.

Chalmer was excited when he walked back into the office. "I'm going to schedule a trip up to the state prison. I've got some questions for Billy Davis and them that guard him."

"Can I go? Uh? Can I?" McIntire pleaded. "I've never been to a real life prison."

"If you're smart, you'll keep it that way!" Chalmer snapped. He immediately wondered why he'd said that. He had no reason to even think McIntire would do anything that was dishonorable. In fact, he had real affection for the lad. He chastised himself for his misdirected anger. Maybe he was more like Pewzer than he thought. Maybe he needed a whipping boy--someone to take his frustration out on. His lack of a resolution to this murder was bearing down on him, and he was getting downright testy.

"Shucks, you know me better than that," McIntire said meekly. I wouldn't hurt a flea on a dog."

Absently, Chalmer responded. "I know that, son."

McIntire was instantly touched by Chalmer's comment. He straightened his shoulders and his chest puffed out. Nobody, not even his own parents, had ever called him son. He had never lived up to their expectations. They were never physically abusive, but he was never smart enough or athletic enough to suit them. But at least they'd provided a roof over his head, and now that he was out of school, they let him stay at their house. However, nothing would have pleased him more than to be the sheriff's son.

Contacting the Warden at the prison and explaining his situation, Chalmer learned that he was welcome to come the next day to talk to a few guards in Billy's cellblock and to Billy himself.

During Chalmer's telephone call, McIntire sat in silence, straining to hear the Warden's loud response. When Chalmer hung up, he pleaded again. "Can I go? Can I?"

The sheriff wanted to say no, but instead said, "Be ready at five o'clock sharp. I want to get an early start. We'll grab some breakfast on the way. In the meantime, why don't you go to the two banks in town and ask them if Mary Davis had a bank account at either place. I'll call the bank in Struthersville." He wanted to know about any money Mary Davis may have deposited from a divorce settlement and if any withdrawals had recently been made.

McIntire was skeptical. "Well shucks, I don't know if they'd give me that information."

Chalmer dug a badge out of his desk drawer and handed it to McIntire. "Here, put that on. That should do it. They'll answer your question." The young deputy's eyes grew wide. He now felt like a real man of the law.

After the inquiries had been made, it was clear that there was no trace of a check being cashed or deposited in area banks by Mary Davis. But the sheriff, as a result of his cordial relationship with Banker Calvin, did find out something even more interesting--that Louella had only yesterday withdrawn a substantial amount of money from Ekbert Pewzer's old account. *She didn't waste any time*, Chalmer concluded. He'd also have to check on any withdrawals from Opal Davis' account. An angry mother might be capable of hiring a killer.

Chapter 35

A WOMAN NAMED IRIS

That evening, Chalmer was getting ready for bed earlier than usual. He needed a good night's sleep before his early-morning drive to the prison. His telephone rang, jolting him. "Hello," he said in a muffled voice.

"Is this Sheriff LeRoy Chalmer?" a pleasant female voice asked.

"Yeah, who wants to know?" the sheriff grumbled, wondering why anyone should be calling him at home about sheriff's business. He shouldn't have had that damn phone put in.

"This is Iris Goodrite."

"So?"

"Well, you see, my dad's a lawyer, and he's pretty good at tracking people down, or at least his people are. I'd say he's more than good. He's very resourceful and has an indomitable spirit. When he makes up his mind to do something, he won't rest until it's done." When Chalmer didn't respond, she went on. "We live in the Chicago area."

Chalmer wasn't impressed. Was she bragging or what? He didn't have any use for sleazy lawyers, and he sure didn't know anybody from Chicago. "So what's your point?" he asked grumpily. "How do I fit into this picture?"

"Well . . . ." She seemed reluctant to go on. "Well, did you once live in an orphanage?"

"As a matter of fact I did, but what's that got to do with you?"

"Well, I did too--for a very short time, that is, before I was adopted by the Goodrites."

When words froze on Chalmer's stunned lips, leaving him unable to say anything, she went on. "Like I said, my dad's pretty good about tracking down things, and when I wanted to know about my birth parents, he pulled some strings and got some sealed records opened up. He found out my birth mother had pinned a name to my sleeper when she left me at the orphanage. The name was Iris Chalmer. He couldn't find out anything about her--not yet anyway. He's still working on that. He did find out I had two brothers, both at the orphanage."

Stunned and still laboring under the shock of this revelation, Chalmer said, "Go on." He was now fully engaged.

"My dad put the word out to look for anybody named Chalmer. It's not a common name, as you well know. As it turned out, one of his associates saw this article in the Springfield newspaper about a Sheriff LeRoy Chalmer investigating a murder case." Her voice grew fainter, less confident, than it had before. "I think you might be my brother."

"Oh?"

"Oh, what?"

"Oh, I'm just surprised, that's all. My brother located me through that same newspaper article just a few days ago." Chalmer had no idea that Pewzer's death could leave so much information in its wake. All because of his murder investigation, he was finding long-lost siblings.

"You've been in touch with him?" she asked excitedly, not even attempting to hide her enthusiasm. "When can I meet with the two of you?"

"Uh, I don't know. Right now I've got pressing sheriff matters--can't be very soon. And as for Josh--that's my brother--he's long gone--don't know where."

"Oh? You didn't stay in touch? Why?"

"That's a long story." Chalmer thought about her dad being a hot-shot lawyer. Perhaps he could help Josh get out of his jam if he ever showed up again, but he said, "Maybe I'll tell ya about it sometime." He had a propensity for being a doubting Thomas, and right now he didn't want to reveal too much. He doubted that her dad could--or would--do much for Josh anyway. He might even turn him over to the law.

"Then when can the two of us get together?"

"Like I said, not for awhile. I've got important sheriff's business to attend to tomorrow--got to go up to the state prison to check on some things."

"What about right now?"

"Now? Well, I thought I'd get to bed early tonight. It's quite a distance up there."

"I'm right here in town. Surely you can take a few minutes to say hello. Meet me at the Daylight Cafe in ten minutes." She hung up.

"What was left for Chalmer to do but to meet this sister he didn't even know he had until a few minutes ago? He pulled his shirt back on, his curiosity thoroughly aroused, and headed to the Daylight Cafe, where he was startled to see this young attractive woman with strawberry blond hair and bright blue eyes sitting in a booth. He couldn't quite believe that she could be his sister, but there were no other women seated alone. He made his way to the booth and introduced himself. She got up and gave him a long embrace. He reluctantly, tentatively, hugged her back, uneasy about what other customers would think. He hoped none of them would recognize him and wonder why a sheriff would be hugging a dignified, elegant woman this late at night, but they seemed to be engrossed in their own private conversations.

Constantly flipping her long tresses away from her smooth ivory face, Iris used impressive words that just came spilling out of her mouth. It was obvious to Chalmer that she had been using them for a very long time. It was for sure she'd been raised in a fancier home than he had been, and it brought back the old insecurity he constantly struggled with. He decided he'd better draw on some of the big words from his notebook--the ones he rehearsed periodically. But soon the two were so engrossed in sharing information that he forgot all about using important-sounding words.

They were soon enthralled with each other's background and what they could learn about family history. They had a lot of catching up to do, and it was midnight, closing time for the cafe, before they left, promising to stay in touch. She reached in her leather clutch purse and searched in vain for something to scribble her phone number and address on. He pulled his little green spiral notebook out of his shirt pocket, turned to a blank page, and handed it to her.

Chapter 36

STATE PRISON

After the sheriff's car cleared the main gate and drove to a parking area designated for special visitors, Chalmer and McIntire made their way toward the warden's office by asking directions of guards on duty. The doors were locked behind them the instant they were slammed shut. McIntire whispered, "Golly durn. This gives me the creeps."

It gave Chalmer the creeps too, but he wasn't about to make any such admission to his deputy. Having been an officer of the law for only a few short years, he had never before stepped foot in the state prison, and somehow this experience rattled him.

The warden, a large man, the kind you'd expect of a warden, welcomed the two visitors, telling them that the prisoners had already eaten their lunch, and he had made arrangements for the sheriff to talk to a couple of guards on Billy's cellblock. But first Chalmer wanted to have a chat with Billy Davis.

He flashed a warning to McIntire. "Keep your mouth shut, and let me do all the talkin'. Understand?" A guard opened Billy's cell door and let the two inside before slamming it shut. The cell was a small cubicle with narrow bunk beds, gray walls, a toilet in one corner, and a rust-covered washbasin.

Inside Billy's cell, Chalmer decided to ask questions as subtly as he could. He'd learned from watching crime shows on television that he shouldn't play his hand too soon. He'd just sort of lead Billy on and let him do the talking. Maybe he'd learn more that way.

"How ya doin', Billy? Are they treatin' ya all right?"

"Yeah, all right, I guess. For a prison anyhow." Billy wasn't what Chalmer expected. Instead of a big strong-looking man who had been raised on a farm, he was a wiry little guy except for the bulging muscles in his otherwise skinny arms. His face was pale, lacking a tan, from too much time inside and not enough out in the sunshine.

"I see ya got big muscles. Ya must get to work out some in here."

"Yeah, we work out when we're outside. We get to go out in the yard in about thirty minutes."

"Well, I won't keep ya from that. I was just wondering if ya have any knowledge of who might have wanted Ekbert Pewzer dead."

"Who didn't! That'd be a better question." Billy eyed Chalmer with suspicion, and when the sheriff didn't say anything else, he said, "You surely don't think I had anything to do with that, do ya? If you'll check, you'll find out that I've been in here since April.

"I know that, Billy."

"Then what do ya want with me?"

"Well, you look like such a nice fella, I can't understand how you'd resort to stealin'."

Billy rolled his eyes up. "Because I was always too proud to beg."

"And not too proud or scared to steal?"

"That's different."

"Oh." Chalmer pondered on that awhile. "I was just wonderin' how often your family comes to visit ya. I'll bet it gets pretty lonesome in here," the sheriff said, in an effort to sound completely sympathetic.

"Sure does, but my mom comes almost every week, and Alvin and Louella come pretty regular."

"What about Alvin's wife? Does she come?"

"Naw, never does."

"Then you're probably not too fond of her?"

"Aw, she's all right. I can't blame her. Why would anybody want to come see somebody in this stinkin' hole?" Billy's demeanor was softening.

"What about Mary's ex-husband. Did he ever come when they were married?"

A strange expression came over Billy's face as if he thought the sheriff might be losing it. Surely he knew more than that. He didn't know what to think. He shook his head. "You've got it all wrong. Mary's never been married. Neither has Louella."

"Oh." Chalmer had just found out what he had been fishing for, and he silently congratulated himself for being so smooth in his duplicity. "By the way, how do ya get along with him?" Chalmer pointed to Billy's cellmate, who was fast asleep on the top bunk, or at least pretended to be.

"Aw, pretty good. He leaves me alone, and I leave him alone."

"Have ya been able to make any friends in here?"

"Naw, not to amount to anything, but I've got to know a few guys pretty good."

"Did your family ever have a chance to meet any of them that are friendly to ya?"

"Naw. Why?"

Chalmer caught a look out of Billy's eyes that seemed to indicate he was suddenly wary and guarded. Billy's reaction had answered his question. "Oh, I was just wonderin'. I thought it might make ya feel less isolated if ya shared some mutual acquaintances."

Billy seemed to relax, falling for Chalmer's white lie and deception.

"Well, I'll leave ya alone. I wouldn't want ya to miss out on that time of yours to get a little fresh air. The weather's a mite cooler today, so enjoy it." He motioned for the guard to open the cell so that he and McIntire could make their exit.

After chatting awhile with one guard and getting nowhere, Chalmer learned from another guard, an affable guy who laughed a lot, that Billy Davis at one time seemed to be chums with a couple of the inmates he worked out with in the yard.

"Where are these guys now?" Chalmer wanted to know.

"They were released about a month ago--got out a few months early for good behavior. But they were just in here for being repeat offenders--partners in petty crimes and the like."

"What are their names?"

"Dennis Jones and Robert Ryan."

"Do ya suppose I could get a picture of 'em somewhere?"

"Well, you'd have to ask the warden about that."

"Sure thing." Chalmer shook the guard's hand and thanked him.

Just then sirens blared. The friendly guard was on full alert and all business. "They must have been one inmate short when they came in from the yard! They're shutting everything down! We're on lockdown until he's found!"

McIntire was horrified. "You mean we can't leave?"

"That's right," the guard yelled over his shoulder as he hastened away to help with the search. "No one comes in or goes out!"

Not knowing what to do with themselves in the midst of the chaos, Chalmer and McIntire watched in fear as people yelled orders, guards hustled about with their weapons drawn, and cells banged shut. Everyone was engaged in the frantic search for the missing inmate.

Finally, Chalmer and McIntire reluctantly made their way back to the hall in which the warden's office was located, found an uncomfortable wooden bench, and waited until the all-clear signal was given.

In a matter of ten-minutes or less, the missing prisoner had been located and returned to his cell.

When Chalmer saw the hands-on warden return to his office, he asked if it was possible for him to get a picture of Dennis Jones and Robert Ryan, explaining that he needed to know what they looked like.

"I'll do better than that," the warden said. "I'll give you a picture and the name of their probation officer. He'll know where they are." His secretary, a tough-looking bleached blonde with a stocky frame, soon produced the pictures and the information. McIntire's eyes rolled and his mouth fell open. It flashed through his mind that she could surely overpower any of the inmates single-handedly.

"Wow, I'm shore glad to get out of there," McIntire uttered as soon as they got in their car and drove back through the gate."

Chalmer gave him a sharp look and got out a map to look up Brownsburg, the town where the probation officer lived. He quelled his desire to chew McIntire out good and proper, but said, "Well, you're the one that wanted to come here, remember?" He studied the map for a few minutes. "It looks like Brownsburg is right on our way. Let's stop in and see if that probation officer can tell us where Jones and Ryan live."

Chapter 37

FORMER INMATES

Located in a small run-down apartment on Fifth Street in Brownsburg, Jones cracked the door open and immediately saw Chalmer's badge. "What do ya want?" the feckless fellow growled. "And how'd ya know where to find me?"

"Well, ya know what they say about the long arm of the law. I just thought I'd ask ya a few questions if ya don't mind."

"Well, I do mind! And I'm not answerin' none of your damn questions. I don't have to, and I'm not goin' to!"

Chalmer stuck his foot on the door stoop when Jones attempted to slam the door shut. "Just one question, that's all. Do ya happen to know any of Billy Davis' family?"

"What's it to ya! I served my time, and I don't have to answer any of your questions, and you damn well sure I won't."

"Well, ya don't have to puff up like a poisoned pup about it, now do ya?" Chalmer made the mistake of shifting his weight, causing his foot to slip off the door stoop. Jones slammed the door shut, catching Chalmer's toes in the process. It hurt like hell. Chalmer looked at the scuffed shoe that he had spit shined just that morning. He detested dirty shoes, and he seethed with anger. He didn't like being treated like a nobody. He and his office deserved more respect than that. In an attempt to calm himself, he took a deep breath and huffed out an explosion of air, right along with some choice swear words. He said to McIntire, "Let's go see if we can find that Ryan fella."

That interview went better. Robert Ryan lived in another run-down apartment on the other end of this small town, but from Ryan's demeanor you'd never know his living quarters were anything but the best. He came to the door twirling a key chain on his finger like he was the most important person in the world. He invited Chalmer and McIntire in as if they were long lost friends and acknowledged that he got to know Billy Davis reasonably well while in prison. But when Chalmer asked him questions about the Davis family, Ryan denied knowing them and assured him that he'd never been to Rothersby or Struthersville. He was slick with that shrewd tongue of his, Chalmer thought. He was the kind that could make you think the sky was green when you knew better. Chalmer couldn't help admiring him for that trait and wished he had some of it himself. It would make his job a lot easier, and maybe it would have made it easier to get along with his ex-wife.

It was dark when the sheriff and his deputy got back into Rothersby. It had been a long day. Chalmer dropped McIntire off at his parents' house and drove to his apartment, still wondering if there had been any connection between these two ex-cons and Pewzer's violent death. He'd take their pictures to Susie's Bar and Grill tomorrow. Maybe the proprietor, who was also the bartender, could identify them. If he could just nail down the killers-for-hire, he'd be half way there.

However, that endeavor the next morning proved fruitless. When the proprietor looked at the pictures of Jones and Ryan, he was unable to ID them. "Naw, I can't say for sure whether they were ever in here or not. But like I said before, the two guys that got Pewzer drunk looked like they were trying to disguise theirselves. I'm here to tell you, if them pictures are of the same men, they sure did a good job of it."

Chalmer took a deep breath and gazed off into space, focusing on the picture of the semi-nude woman behind the bar. Another dead end! He was stumped, and just when he thought he was getting somewhere!

Chapter 38

THE DECISION

Chalmer only had time to get back to his apartment and go to the bathroom, when the doorbell rang. It was Sally again. "Now, LeRoy, why don't you get a telephone? It would make things a lot simpler. I wouldn't have had to drive all the way over here."

"If it's anything to you, I already got one," came his curt reply with his bristled defenses immediately coming into play. When she started a sentence with *Now, LeRoy*, it was a red flag. She'd often used his first name just to provoke him. He used to shutter at that, knowing full well that it was the beginning of some order or some complaint, or something else she didn't approve of. And who was she to tell him what to do!

"That's all the more reason you should seriously consider my proposition," she cooed. "You have thought about it, haven't you-- like you said you would. You wouldn't have to pay the whole cost of a telephone bill, now would you?"

He had thought about it, and it did make sense, considering how much it cost to keep up two different living quarters. Pooling their resources would help out, but living together would prove more advantageous to her since she earned such a little amount of money, but then again, he wouldn't have to make those dratted alimony payments. His sheriff's pay wasn't anything to brag about. Bitterly, he was reminded again about his paycheck. It was so stingy that you'd think it came out of the county judges' own pockets.

"Yeah, I've thought about it." Hovering on the brink of indecision, he frowned and rubbed his lower lip as if deep in thought. "But I haven't made up my mind yet." He didn't much like dickering around, but he realized that no matter what his decision, it had the possibility of being filled with regrets.

"Well, what's keeping you? Surely, you can see that it'd be a good thing for both of us." He looked at his ex. She was dressed in a hip-hugging white skirt and a blue blouse with a scooped neckline. Old emotions stirred, and it suddenly hit him with a heart-stopping thud just how much he still loved her. He wanted to take her to bed, the way it used to be when they were first married and so much in love.

He shook that thought from his head and murmured, "Aren't ya afraid of what people would think--with us not bein' married anymore?"

"I hadn't thought much about that. Remember, we'll just be sharing the same roof, not living like man and wife. What's wrong with that?"

"Nothin', I guess, but then other people wouldn't know that, would they?"

"Let them think what they want. After all we were married for fifteen years, even if they were pretty miserable sometimes."

"And who's fault was that?" he asked with a sharp, penetrating gaze.

"Well, whose do you think?"

"I suppose that depends upon which one of us you're talkin' to."

"Well, that's neither here nor there. What will it be?" She clamped her lips together, stared him straight in the eyes, and waited for a response. When none came, she added, "I need to know. My utility bills are coming due, and I need to know if I'll have to come up with all the money for them. And besides, there's a leak under the kitchen sink. You know I'm not good at things like that, and it's your house too. You wouldn't want it to ruin the floor, would you?"

Another red flag! Chalmer knew deep down in his heart that he shouldn't fall for her bait, but it was an intriguing offer. In spite of everything, he still loved her. Why? He didn't know, but love is as hard to shake as ticks off a dog's back. As she waited for his response, Chalmer's bravado dissolved and he became vulnerable to memories and loneliness. With a glimmer of hope, he speculated that it might just work, and he finally acquiesced. "I guess we can try it for a while and see how things work out."

"Good, I'll make room for you in the extra bedroom. When will you be there?"

"This afternoon, I suppose. Just might as well get it done."

That afternoon LeRoy Chalmer packed his few items of clothing, his toiletries, and some other personal items. He wouldn't take much. He'd have to see how things went, and he wouldn't sublease his apartment either. He decided to keep it a bit longer--just in case.

Sally greeted him at the door and helped him carry in his meager belongings. When they deposited the items on the bed in the spare bedroom, Chalmer had a strange expression on his face. He'd never paid much attention to this tiny room, and it was to be his sleeping quarters. Sally, of course, would occupy the big bedroom, the one they used to share and make love in. He was struck with a sudden bout of renewed sadness. How had his life come to this? He hoped he hadn't made a mistake, or maybe a pact with the devil. What a thought! He was ashamed for even toying with such an idea.

That night, he discovered that the mattress was lumpy, allowing little sleep on his part. He tossed and fretted all night, and when he did sleep, he was bothered with those recurring dreams that had to do with his investigation of Pewzer's death.

The next morning was awkward. Sally wasn't up yet. She was a late sleeper, and now that she worked as a hostess during the dinner hour at a local restaurant a couple of evenings a week, she got home late and was accustomed to sleeping well into the morning. After getting dressed, Chalmer went to the kitchen and fixed a pot of coffee--a familiar routine. He repaired the leak under the kitchen sink. He'd grab something to eat on the way to the office. But right now, he needed a cigarette.

He had just taken a few long drags off his Marlboro when Sally came screeching and stumbling into the kitchen. "What do you think you're doing? I could smell the smoke all the way in the bedroom. If you're going to smoke, do it outside! Understand?" She did an about-face and stormed back into the bedroom with a jarring bang of the door.

"What have I done?" Chalmer muttered under his breath. He should have known it would be like this. He never seemed to learn from past mistakes.

That morning, he testified in court concerning yet another domestic assault. Would people never learn to get along? He thought about Sally. Sometimes he'd like to do a little punching on his own. Testifying was the part of his job that he detested. He never felt he was articulate enough, and he hated being questioned by lawyers, who always seemed to have sophisticated tongues that tried to cross him up.

When he got home that evening, it was still scorching hot. Sally was ready for work--dressed in a low-cut blouse and a tight-fitting skirt. Her hair gleamed, a perfect frame for her carefully applied makeup and bright red lipstick, and her eyes had a sultry look about them. Her swaying hips almost made Chalmer's head spin, and he couldn't take his eyes off her. He yearned to take her to bed. What man wouldn't? She was an invitation all wrapped up in a delectable package, even if she was a little too heavy. But then, he wondered just what she was trying to catch at that restaurant--probably another man.

She sashayed toward the door. "Oh, by the way, LeRoy, the lawn needs mowing. You'll have plenty of time to get it done before dark. And don't forget to trim the hedge."

Chalmer's hopes for a reconciliation plummeted. He realized without a single doubt that he had been hood-winked again, and he bristled. He was angrier with himself than he was with her. How could he have been so utterly stupid?

After she was gone, Chalmer dug his heels in, went to the bedroom, and repacked his meager belongings. The arrangement, if you could call it that, would never work. Would he never learn? How many times would it take? He cursed himself as he loaded his things into the sheriff's car. It was already stifling hot, and he was steaming from anger.

When he drove away from his former home, he glanced at the redbud tree spreading its heart-shaped leaves to provide a good shade. He had planted it years ago. He also looked at the lawn and the hedge. "I wonder what fool she'll get to take care of that," he breathed aloud in a pinched whisper. "Probably some lover or someone she's able to tease into it. At least it won't be me." Oddly, he didn't feel any remorse--or any of his old love for Sally--only relief and anger. He'd always heard that there was a fine line between love and hate, and now he believed it. He promised himself he wouldn't let that love return and that he was done with her for good. Maybe that was just wishful thinking, but he sincerely hoped not.

Chapter 39

A LONG-AGO MOM

"Oh, LeRoy, I've got wonderful news!" came the voice over the phone.

It took Chalmer a few minutes for it to register in his brain that it was Iris, his sister. "Oh, what's that?"

"I've found our mother!"

"You what?" Chalmer couldn't believe what she was saying. "What do ya mean? You mean our birth mother?"

"Yes, that's exactly what I mean."

"Uh, how did all that happen?"

"Well, I told you my dad was good at tracking down things, and he and his associates found her."

Chalmer wasn't sure he wanted to hear any of this, but he asked, "Uh, where is she?"

"Her name's Dorothy Ellis. She's in a nursing home, and you won't believe this, but she's not far from where you live--less than a two-hour drive. And it's really not all that far from where I live--farther than you, but not too far." Iris was so excited that she was breathless.

"Well, I'll be a monkey's uncle." He felt stupid for saying such a thing, but he was too shocked to come up with a good response.

"You'll be a what?"

"Oh, never mind. That's just a silly saying."

"Aren't you excited?"

"Well, I suppose so, but I hadn't thought anything about her for such a long time. I guess in my mind she just didn't exist anymore. I guess I'm more surprised than anything else."

"Well, LeRoy, she does exist, and aren't you curious to know about her?"

"Yeah. Yeah, I'm curious--kinda anyway."

"Then let's meet at that nursing home and go see her."

"You're kidding--right?"

"No, I'm not. I'm dead serious. How about it?"

"Well, I don't know about that. I'm pretty busy right now. You know with a murder investigation and all."

"Too busy to go see your own mother!"

"Well, she doesn't seem like any mother to me, and why would she to you?"

"Because . . . because I've got to know. Tell me you'll meet me there tomorrow."

He hedged. He didn't want to go. "No, I don't think that'd be a very good idea."

"Then what am I supposed to tell her when I go see her--that her own son didn't want to have anything to do with her?"

Chalmer knew what her tactic was. She was trying to send him on a guilt trip, and she was doing a pretty good job of it. Why couldn't he just stand up for himself and not let people do this to him? "Well, when I was just a kid, she didn't want to have anything to do with me. Just tell her what you want."

"Oh, come on. You have to be curious. You are, aren't you?"

"Yeah, I suppose so, but like I said, I'm pretty busy right now."

"Too busy to take just one day off? And it wouldn't be fair to let me go alone. I need you for moral support. Please say yes."

That did it for Chalmer. How could he say no to a lady in distress? He hesitated, his silence hanging in the air, before saying, "Oh, all right. Tell me where this nursing home is and how to get there, and what time you want me there."

"Have you got a piece of paper?"

"Sure." He pulled his notebook out of his shirt pocket and began to write.

Chalmer knew he would be creating a volatile situation, but he had to ask Sally for her car. He couldn't very well drive the sheriff's car on any personal business that would require a two-hour drive. He drove toward his former home and immediately spotted the car in the driveway.

Sally exploded when he told her in a congenial way that he needed the car. "What do you need my car for? I have to have it to get to work!" she screeched.

That ended the congeniality. So much for being nice! "Well, if you remember right, it's my car too--still got my name on the title and I'm still making payments on it!" he fired back. "Besides, I intend to go visit the woman who gave birth to me." He couldn't quite bring himself to use the word *mother* or *mom*. "She's in a nursing home up in Denton County."

"When did all this come about! LeRoy Chalmer, you're lying to me, and I know it! You don't know anything about your real mother! So don't try to concoct a story like that! Do you think I'm stupid!"

"For your information, I'm not concocting anything, and I'm not lying, and I want the car." He was exacerbated now, but his voice softened to clarify his intentions. "Just for one day. You can take a cab if ya need to go some place." He didn't think she was stupid, but she was something far worse. She was a bitch--a certified bitch.

"And what if I won't let you have it?" she spat out.

"Then I'll take it anyway." He was through with being nice. "They can't very well arrest a man for taking his own car." He got out his car keys--the ones that still dangled from his key chain. "Try and stop me."

Chalmer stood transfixed as he looked at the frail, salt-and-pepper haired woman, who sat in a wheelchair. She had dark circles under her blue eyes and looked to be in her sixties or perhaps early seventies. Deep wrinkles creased her face. Was he supposed to feel something? He didn't. Not a thing. Surrounded by the smell of a nursing home--predominately urine, he could hardly take a deep breath. He was glad he didn't have to live in a place like this, if you could call it living.

He looked at Iris. She was handling this much better than he was. "I don't know whether they told you we were coming to visit you. They were supposed to, but we're your daughter and your son--the ones you gave . . . you were forced to leave at an orphanage. This is LeRoy Chalmer and I'm Iris Goodrite."

Tears welled up in Dorothy Ellis' eyes before splashing down her pale, withered cheeks. The silence then was interminable, unbearably so.

Chalmer felt uneasy and wished he hadn't come. What do you say to a mother you couldn't remember, one that had abandoned you? He wished Josh were here. What would he say? What does this stranger of a woman say? What *could* she say?

Finally, Iris broke the silence. It wasn't as hard for her. She'd had a better life, and it was easier for her to take all this in, to come to grips with it. Her childhood had been better than his or Josh's. A wonderful one. Being abandoned had probably been a blessing for her. Not so for him or Josh. Iris was curious, and she needed answers. "Do you feel like talking?"

Dorothy nodded. "Yes, I'd like to explain everything. I don't want either of you to think I'm a monster. I'm really not, you know."

"Then we'd like to hear all about it." Iris spoke in a soft, understanding voice.

"The two of you had different fathers." She looked at LeRoy. "When I was a freshman in college, I fell in love with Keith Chalmer, dropped out of school, and got married. I gave birth to you and Josh--if that's still his first name. We had a good life--nothing extra, but we were happy." She sniffled and looked away. "But then tragedy struck. Keith was killed in a construction accident. He worked for a company that built apartments." Her voice trailed off, but she soon recovered. "That's been a long time ago, but I had no way of supporting the two of you. I couldn't get a job with two young boys to take care of. I tried, but we were kicked out of our apartment when I couldn't pay the rent, and we ended up living in a roach-infested place that was in a dangerous part of town. It was nothing but squalor. I knew I couldn't let you boys live like that--if you'd have survived at all, so I left you at the orphanage." With tears streaming down her face, she choked up. And so did LeRoy, but he tried his best to hide his emotions as he listened to her tell about the hardships she had endured. "I was devastated and cried every night, tormented about what might be happening to you, but there wasn't a thing I could do."

Her eyes then shifted to Iris. "Several years later, I met your father--Bill Timmerman, fell in love again, and married him. You were born within a year, and we were happy--until I told him about my two boys. I should have told him before we were married, but couldn't bring myself to talk about it. I told him I wanted to go back to that orphanage and bring them to live with us if they were still there. He blew up and said he hadn't bargained to raise somebody else's brats. That's what he said. He walked out, and I haven't seen him since. When I left you at the orphanage, I wrote the name Chalmer on your little sleeper so you'd have a connection to your half-brothers. All of you needed to know you were family and not alone." As if trying to shake away the bad memory of giving up her children, she slowly extended her arthritic hand away from her breast where it had been since starting her revelation. It seemed to be a gesture that pleaded for their understanding and forgiveness.

"But your name's Ellis. That made it hard to find you. Did you marry again after my . . . uh, my father left?"

"Yes. Just a few years ago. He was old, and I was his housekeeper. But I was more than that. I took care of him--more like a nurse. He was good to me and wanted to marry me, and I said yes. But he died soon afterward. His kids got the house and what little money he had. He hadn't changed his will. Then I got sick, and here I am, a ward of the court."

Just listening to her made Chalmer sorrowful, but he was impressed with how articulate she was. Looking at her frail body, he could hardly imagine that her mind was so sharp.

She wanted to know all about their lives--if it had been good, where they lived, what they did, where Josh was--all the usual things. Each of them filled her in before they had to leave, with Iris telling the absolute truth and LeRoy sugar coating his life in a foster home and Josh's young life spent in the orphanage. He didn't tell her that Josh was running from the law.

Iris had one more question of her own. "Do you have any idea where Bill Timmerman is now--even where he might have gone?"

"Why on earth would you care?"

"Because . . . just because," Iris replied pensively. She had an over-riding desire to trace her roots. It had become a compulsion, and she just couldn't help it.

Dorothy rolled her eyes to one side. "I don't know. Don't have any idea. But he was originally from Kentucky. Maybe that would help."

Iris thanked her, bent down, and gave her an affectionate hug--a genuine one. LeRoy hoped he wasn't expected to do the same, but when Dorothy held out her arms to him, what could he do? He halfheartedly squeezed her shoulders and patted her softly on the back. It gave him a strange, unsettling feeling.

"I'm so glad I finally got to meet up with both of you again. I just wish I could've seen Josh," she whispered. "But I can die in peace now. They tell me I don't have long." LeRoy felt a great sadness stir within him for this woman who had given birth to him. How strange it was that Ekbert Pewzer had done him a favor. If not for his investigation of the man's murder, neither Josh nor Iris would have ever found him and contacted him. And he would never have known his birth mother or that his father was a good man who had died--or that his mother and father had loved him in spite of what he had always believed and had always haunted him.

Outside, he thanked Iris, whom he now knew to be his half-sister, and once again told her to stay in touch. He said goodbye and got in the car, eager to get it back to Sally, who would demand that he tell her about his birth mother, just to make sure he hadn't lied to her. He had already made up his mind to tell her absolutely nothing.

Chapter 40

A FUNERAL PROCESSION

In his office the next day, Chalmer flipped through the pages of the local newspaper with special interest in the obituary section. Just as he suspected, Mary Davis' death notice was recorded there. Her funeral was to be at the Struthersville Baptist Church and burial in the only cemetery near that small town. She would be laid to rest in the same hallowed grounds that Ekbert Pewzer had been buried. Somehow that seemed fitting to Chalmer.

He wanted to be there when the funeral procession made its way to the cemetery. But first he needed to have another chat with the whittler, his ubiquitous source of information. Maybe he had something new to report. Chalmer told McIntire to hold down the fort at the office before he began the familiar trip to Struthersville.

There he found the whittler in his usual spot in front of the barbershop and across the street from Phillips' store. This was an ideal spot for seeing everything that went on in Struthersville's Main Street. By this time, he had established a good rapport with the informative old man, who seemed to trust him enough to fill him in on his hunches as well as the facts. The information was sometimes slow in coming, but it eventually made its way through the whittler's lips.

"Hello, Snellings. How's it goin'?"

Pewzer's Wake

"Aw, pretty good, I reckon. Can't complain none. This breeze shore is nice. How's it goin' with you? Are ya any closer to solvin' your case?"

"Naw, not much." He looked down at Snellings. "It seems I'm always runnin' in to dead ends. I thought you might have some new information for me. Maybe you've thought of somethin' else or heard somethin' else. I know how good ya are about watchin' and listenin'."

"Well, as a matter of fact, I did think of somethin'."

Chalmer's eyes brightened. "Oh, what's that?"

"Ya know I was tellin' ya about how Lyle is deaf and dumb? Well, some people don't know how good he can read lips, and he's really anything but dumb. And he can talk--not too plain--but he can talk good enough. They say he was about six when he came down with some disease that made him deaf, but he'd already learned to talk." He again pronounced the word *deaf* with a long *e*.

Chalmer wanted the whittler to get to the point, but he knew he had to show restraint. Snellings would take his own sweet time, and he couldn't be rushed.

"Well, I just remembered somethin'."

"What was that?"

Just then the funeral procession on the way to the cemetery came into view. The whittler fell silent out of respect, and the sheriff felt he had to do the same.

Following the hearse that carried Mary Davis' remains, Opal and Louella rode in the Rothersby mortuary limousine. Alvin Davis and his family followed in their car. Other than that, the short procession consisted of no more than eight or ten other cars, presumably bearing close friends or coworkers of the family. Apparently prison authorities had not released Billy Davis long enough to attend the funeral of his sister.

The whittler just kept whittling and didn't follow up on the story he had started. He seemed to be deep in thought. Chalmer knew him well enough to know that he couldn't be rushed--that he'd take his own sweet time. Wondering just what might be in that head of the whittler, he sat down next to him, watching the shavings of a stick fall to the ground, almost mesmerizing him.

When the funeral procession was out of sight and made the slow curve toward the cemetery, Chalmer prompted the whittler to continue, "And you were saying?" The whittler remained silent. Chalmer knew he would talk when he got good and ready, and not a minute before. It was a long wait--a wait that made the sheriff wonder if he was wasting time, but then he came to the conclusion that his time wasn't all that precious anyway. After the burial, Alvin and his family drove back through town on their way back home. After hugging Louella, her only remaining daughter, and uttering a tearful goodbye, Opal Davis settled back in the limousine for the ride back to Rothersby, where Chalmer assumed she had left her car.

Sadly, Louella, in a snug-fitting black sheath dress appropriate for mourning, stood waving goodbye until the limousine was out of sight. She was visibly upset as tears streamed down her face. Chalmer couldn't help liking Louella almost as much as the hormone-driven McIntire did, only in a different sort of way. He wasn't good at delivering condolences, but nevertheless, he crossed the street, approached her and said uncomfortably, "Louella, I'm sorry for your loss."

That act of kindness prompted an even greater demonstration of grief. She flung her arms around him and broke down in great sobs. Gasping for air and stretching out the words, she wailed, "Oh, sheriff, I don't know if I can live without Mary. She was everything to me. When we were kids, she protected me from Ekbert the best she could. She was the only one who truly understood what I was going through, and now she's gone. It's just not fair. It's not right. Right now, my heart's so heavy--all weighted down by sorrow, but it continues to beat on and on. Oh, sheriff, how can I bear it?"

Chalmer had always had a soft spot in his heart for a weeping woman--even if the tears were phony. He couldn't help it. Responding to her show of affection, he wrapped his arms around her in a fatherly way and sputtered, "Do ya want me to drive ya over to your house?" His worried voice changing, becoming sadly thoughtful, he said, "It's no trouble at all." His lack of confidence was there again, his old misgivings about how little he measured up. With his inadequate feeling nagging at him, he just didn't know how to rise to the occasion, and he didn't know what else to say. He didn't know if Louella was faking it or not, but if she was, she was certainly doing a fantastic job of it and was definitely convincing.

He felt his body going from warm to hot. He was a sucker when it came to women. He hoped he wasn't being one at this moment and making a big fool of himself, because he had a pretty strong suspicion that she was the one who had paid somebody to have that rotten Pewzer done it. The thought disturbed him, but from the beginning, he had pursued every possible option and had finally narrowed his list of suspects down to just a few people--one of them being Louella.

She sniffed and wiped her nose with the dainty white handkerchief clutched in her hand. "No thanks. The walk'll do me good. Physical activity always helps. Anyway, I need to get a loaf of bread and something for my lunch." She looked at him with red-rimmed eyes that could melt the coldest snow, and especially Chalmer's fickle heart. "I have to go back to work tomorrow, but I appreciate your kindness," she said, still sobbing and wiping her nose.

"Then take care of yourself," he said as he turned to walk back across the street to sit with the whittler, who looked as if he might be ready to talk.

"And you were saying?" Chalmer prompted Snellings.

"Oh, yeah. I thought of the time Lyle seemed to be understandin' a conversation between the two girls--ya know, that one you was just talkin' to and the one that was just buried. I reckon they didn't know he could read lips. Anyhow, his jaw sorta dropped at somethin' they said. It kinda seemed to shock him."

"Do ya suppose I ought to go have a little chat with him?"

"Well, I know if I was in your shoes, I'd be curious enough to do just that."

"Then I think I'll mosey down to the end of the street. You did say they lived in that little white house, didn't ya?" Chalmer said, pointing to a dilapidated structure which was badly in need of repair.

"Shore thing." The whittler absently ran a finger over a mole on his face. "Sheriff, I'd be interested in hearin' about what ya find out, if it's not too much trouble."

"Sure thing. You're always a great help."

Chapter 41

LYLE, THE DEAF MAN

Burk cracked the door open barely enough for the sheriff to peek in. "What do ya want? I know you're the sheriff, and I didn't do nothing. Honest, I didn't, and Lyle didn't either." His wrinkled face, bloodshot eyes, and waddle neck reflected anxiety and real fear.

Chalmer was surprised at how nervous he was. You would have thought somebody was going to beat him up or arrest him, or maybe kill him. "I know ya didn't, Burk," he said softly, in an attempt to assuage his misgivings. "I know you're a good man, and I've heard how good ya are to take care of your brother there." He could see Lyle sitting on one end of an old divan that had exposed springs sticking up from the dirty, brown upholstery. The rest of the small room wasn't furnished much better, and Chalmer could hardly believe it when he detected an appetizing smell coming from the tiny lean-to kitchen. "Is it all right if I come in?" He tried to talk pleasantly, softly, in a way that wasn't intimidating. "I just wanted to talk to Lyle, if it's all right."

Burk opened the door just wide enough to let Chalmer squeeze in.

"What smells so good?" Chalmer asked. Surely, this baloney-eating fellow didn't cook.

"Oh, that there's a squirrel that Miss Wilson brought over. She does that sometimes when her husband kills an old squirrel. She boils 'em real good for us. She's a real nice woman."

"Well, I'd say she must be. There's nothin' like a good squirrel, is there?" Chalmer thought how much better a young fried squirrel would be than an old boiled one, but it seemed to be a real treat for these two who lived so meagerly, probably on a skimpy old-age pension. It was considerate of this Wilson lady to cook anything for them. He admired her even though he didn't even know her.

Still nervous, Burk asked, "What do ya want to talk to Lyle about?"

"Oh, something he might have heard in town."

"Lyle don't hear nothing. He's deaf." Burk also pronounced the word *deaf* with a long *e*.

"That's what I understand, but somebody told me that he reads lips real good. Is that right?"

"Yeah, when he has a mind to."

"Well, anyway, I'd like to ask him a question or two."

Burk nodded in Lyle's direction. "Ya can set over there in that chair where he can see your lips."

Chalmer eased himself into the rickety wooden rocker, and in a gesture of friendship, reached over and patted Lyle's frail arm, which he quickly withdrew. It was clear that the white-haired Lyle was standoffish and didn't like to be touched.

"Lyle," Chalmer started, confused about just how simple he had to keep his language and how carefully he needed to mouth the words so that Lyle could read his lips. "Someone in town told me that you know about a conversation--that you heard--that you saw two women talking. The women were Mary Davis and Louella Pewzer. Do you remember that?"

Lyle's squinted, rheumy eyes darted apprehensively toward Burk. Chalmer wasn't sure that he had understood what had been said. He seemed frightened, but Burk nodded as if giving the okay for Lyle to answer the question.

"Yeah, I did." Lyle's speech was hesitant and somewhat unclearly enunciated.

"And can you tell me what they were talkin' about?"

Lyle stared across the room and nodded his head ever so slightly, giving permission for Chalmer to continue.

"What did they say?"

"One said she had that man killed."

"Which one was that?"

"The youngest one."

"You mean Louella?"

"Yeah, that's what I mean."

"Are you sure it wasn't Mary who said she'd paid somebody to have the man killed?" Chalmer tried to speak clearly while forming the words slowly and carefully. He didn't want any mistakes or misunderstandings.

"Naw, it tweren't Mary. I know her. She was always nice to me."

"And what else did they say? I've got to be real sure about this."

"Mary said not to worry about it. She said she'd take care of it. She said she didn't have long to live anyhow. That made me sad. I liked her."

"What do you think she meant when she said she'd take care of it?"

"She said she'd say that she did it, and nobody could prove anything different."

"You're sure of that?"

"If I wasn't sure, I wouldn't be sayin' it, now would I?" He stumbled on his words. "I didn't want to talk to you anyhow. You won't tell anybody I told you, will ya?"

"No, Lyle, I won't tell anyone."

That's when Burk, who had remained silent while standing off to one side of the bleak room, intervened. "Promise us that ya won't."

"I promise. Cross my heart, I promise."

Both Burk and Lyle seemed to relax for the first time since Chalmer had arrived. "Well, thanks for your help," he said while rising from the squeaky chair that he thought might collapse under his weight when he pushed himself up. "I appreciate it. I'll be goin' now and leave ya alone."

Chapter 42

A STRONG SENSE OF DUTY

On the drive back to his office, Chalmer churned over in his mind all that he had learned, but it seemed to sour his stomach. He reached in his pocket for a cigarette and leaned over the steering wheel long enough to light it. After taking a few puffs, he snuffed it out in the ashtray.

He didn't want to believe what he had suspected all along and now knew to be true. He should arrest Louella, force her to give him the names of the men she had hired to kill Pewzer, and charge her with first-degree murder. But he had a problem with that. He felt sorry for her, now that Mary had died and carried her secret to the grave. It was buried with her, and he couldn't prove otherwise. In fact, he couldn't prove much of anything. He couldn't involve Lyle. He'd made a promise, and besides, what jury would believe a guy like that anyway?

He wrestled with his conscience. It was his sworn duty to uphold the law. Sure, it was his duty, all right, but somehow, duty just didn't seem to be enough at this particular moment. The more he thought about it, the more he sweated and fretted about what he should do. With steaming hot air blowing in the car's windows, why wouldn't he be uncomfortable? He tried to convince himself that it wasn't his torment over his obligation as a sheriff that made him sweat so profusely. It was the heat, this damn sweltering heat! He reached up and pulled his collar away from his neck, twisting his neck to one side as he did so.

He shifted his position enough to pull a handkerchief out of his hip pocket so he could wipe his brow. When he got right down to it, what difference did it make that Ekbert Pewzer was beaten do death? Nobody cared. Everybody was glad to be rid of him and all the bullying he had always left in his wake. Anybody that knew him thought whoever had killed him had done a great service for the whole area. Justice had already been served. Anyway, he'd never be able to pin the brutal slaying on anybody. It was anything but a slam-dunk case.

He felt sure that Louella had paid Jones and Ryan, Billy's fellow inmates, to bash Pewzer's head in, but there was no way he could prove it. As Mary had said, the killers were long gone, or at least out of the picture. He couldn't prove a thing. Yet, it bothered him that he was even questioning what to do. Being a man of the law, it was his duty to charge the suspects. But then again, even if a prosecutor resisted Louella's charms and brought the case to trial, which was unlikely, any jury that consisted of just a few men would never declare a guilty verdict against such a seductive woman--one that could turn the charm on at the drop of a hat.

When he stepped out of the late afternoon's heat and into his air-conditioned office, McIntire was there waiting for him and couldn't quite contain himself until he was filled in. "Did ya find out anything new?" he asked.

"Yeah, unfortunately, I found out a lot."

"What do ya mean, unfortunately? I thought that's what ya wanted."

"Yeah, I know." He tapped a smoke out of an almost empty pack and fingered the unlit cigarette. "I know," he repeated, "but I didn't find out what I *wanted* to find out."

McIntire looked confused. "I don't get it."

"Well, I found out for sure that it was Louella who paid somebody to have Pewzer killed."

McIntire didn't much like the sound of that. He thought Louella was one hot babe with her sexy clothes and an even sexier voice. He couldn't quite picture her in prison and in a prison uniform--especially not after seeing the state prison for men. It just didn't seem right to lock up a pretty thing like that, let alone deprive an awful lot of men of all the ogling she created. "How'd ya find out it was her?"

"I'll tell ya some other time. Right now, I'm too tired to talk about it." He didn't even want to think about it, much less talk about it.

McIntire didn't let Chalmer's comment deter him. He was even more curious now. He didn't give up that easily and pushed for answers. "What do ya plan to do about it?" he asked, dreading what he was about to hear.

"Nothin', that's what."

"Nothin'! What do ya mean?"

"Exactly what I said," the sheriff snapped. He didn't like being questioned--especially not by his young deputy, the one that was still no more than a kid. "Nothin'. Do I have to spell it out for ya? N-O-T-H-I-N-G!"

Though relieved, McIntire still couldn't quite get it through his thick head. "But ya just now said that she did it--or anyways at least paid to get it done."

"Yeah, I did."

"Then?"

"Then the case is closed. That's all there is to it. Can't ya get that through your thick head! I have a confession, don't I? One that Mary made and took to her grave. And Pewzer can't be any deader or one bit more deservin' of what he got, can he?"

"But ya said ya didn't believe Mary's confession."

"Yeah, yeah, I know, but like I said, case closed, and that's the end of it, and you'd be wise to keep your yap shut."

Chalmer leaned back in his chair, lit his Marlboro, and blew smoke rings in a gesture of self-congratulation and self-satisfaction. A smile tugged at the corner of his mouth. The long arm of the law wasn't so long after all.